They were identical...

The three golden-haired heads bent over the playhouse—Brady, his uncle and Max. Three generations of Morgan males swam in front of her eyes as surely as if an artist had painted them there.

Jenny's heart pounded and she struggled to catch her breath. Suddenly there were answers to the puzzling questions that had lingered in the back of her mind. The similar smiles, the similar walk...

The clues had all been there, right in front of her eyes. But she'd allowed her desire for Brady to cloud her vision. The way he'd held her, run his hands over her body as if she'd belonged to him... The man must have been a consummate actor to have played such a convincing role. And she'd almost believed she loved him.

Before he could look up, she backed away and ran to her office as if the devil was hard at her heels. She'd been warned, she thought wildly as tears welled in her eyes. It was a one-in-a-million shot— but Max's father had found him!

Mollie Molay

LIKE FATHER, LIKE SON

Harlequin Books

TORONTO • NEW YORK • LONDON
AMSTERDAM • PARIS • SYDNEY • HAMBURG
STOCKHOLM • ATHENS • TOKYO • MILAN
MADRID • WARSAW • BUDAPEST • AUCKLAND

To the memory of Joe Molé,
who taught me how to laugh.
And to my wonderful editor, Debra Matteucci,
who understands the value of laughter.
Thank you.

ISBN 0-373-16638-9

LIKE FATHER, LIKE SON

Copyright © 1996 by Mollie Molé.

Chapter One

A rumbling awakened her. Fearful in the pitch-blackness, she reached for the digital clock. It was 4:00 a.m.

Suddenly the bed shook. The light on the clock disappeared. Glass splintered. A table crashed. The whole house trembled. Earthquake! Dear Lord, was this the big one? Horrified, she clung to the bed while framed pictures bounced off the bedroom walls and dresser drawers slid open with a scream of shattering wood.

"Mommy!" a young voice wailed.

Heart pounding, she jumped out of bed and crossed the hall to her son's room.

"Mommy, Mommy!"

Max's muffled voice quivered with terror as he huddled beneath the blankets. Piteous little barks told her the new puppy, Duke, was seeking shelter under the covers with Max.

She gathered her four-year-old son in her arms. "It's okay, sweetheart. It's okay. Mommy is here." Her voice cracked as she fought to control her panic. "It's an earthquake. We'll go downstairs, just as we practiced for our earthquake drill. Remember?''

"Okay." Max sobbed as he burrowed more closely into his mother's arms. "But we're not practicing now, are we?''

"No. But we know what to do, don't we?''

There was an eerie silence. The rolling abruptly stopped. Now the only things she could hear were Max's sobs, Duke's whimpering and her own rapid breath. Duke scrambled into her lap. She smelled dust and plaster and fear. She grabbed a blanket and groped for Max's Ninja Turtle slippers beside the bed. "Let's go downstairs." Her voice quavered; she'd never been *so* afraid.

Downstairs! From the sound of falling objects she was afraid what she would find. All of a sudden there was another violent shake, then another, until with a massive shudder the movement finally stopped. She tried to turn on the lamp beside the bed; the power was out.

Quickly, anxiously, with Max in her arms and Duke sliding at her heels, Jenny gingerly felt her way downstairs.

As she made her way to the front door, additional shocks shook the house. Outside, neighbors stood in the street. Flashlight beams broke the darkness.

"Hey, everyone!" an unknown voice shouted. "Turn off your gas lines before we have a fire!"

Jenny stood paralyzed. Turn off the gas lines? She'd practiced doing it in daylight, but it was dark now. How would she find the pipes and the wrench?

"Oh, my God! The power is off," another voice yelled. "There are no telephones to call for help, either!"

Jenny clasped Max closer as she saw water cascading from the garage. The water heater must have broken! She glanced at her feet—in her panic she'd forgotten to put on shoes.

"Here, Jenny," her next-door neighbor said to her. "I left a pair of running shoes outside yesterday. Put them on before you cut yourself."

"Thanks, Hank," Jenny replied gratefully. Times like this made her realize how much people needed one another.

If things were this bad here, she thought with a sinking heart, how damaged would the small day-care center she operated be? Worse yet, where would the children go until the building was safe? So many of them were the children of working single mothers, and needed her to comfort them, to give them a sense of security.

But who was there to make her feel secure?

BRADY MORGAN cursed when he saw the condition of his office. Bookcases had toppled; papers, books and precious journals lay scattered over the desk and floor. He was in Denver when the earthquake struck, and had come home to Los Angeles to find the buildings and his office a mess. Television news hadn't exaggerated the damage from the quake that had rocked the area three days ago.

He gathered loose papers and stacked them on the desk to be sorted. Books with broken backs he set aside for repair. The others he placed in secure bookcases. Thank goodness, he thought with a deep sigh of relief, his latest research journals were still securely locked in the office safe. Unconsciously, he turned on the small television that sat beside his desk. More earthquake news. Somehow he couldn't get enough of it.

His attention was drawn by the sound of a woman's voice as she was being interviewed. It was low and musical, and surprisingly upbeat in spite of her damaged surroundings.

"So, you're the operator of this day-care center, Miss Walker?" The camera panned over a small building. Its doors hung loose and glass from its shattered windows was strewn over the concrete driveway. Roof tiles littered the playground and several small tricycles lay toppled beside a slide that had tipped over on its side.

"Yes, I am," the woman responded ruefully as she looked around her. "It was a miracle the quake happened before the children arrived. Thank goodness for earthquake insurance. Hopefully, the building will be repaired as quickly as possible and we can reopen. The children desperately need to return to school and get back to normal."

"Don't we all," the newswoman rejoined. "I think I know just how they feel. But surely they have parents who can care for them, and homes of their own?"

"Not all of them." The owner of the school smiled sadly. "Most of our children come from single-parent homes with working mothers. Children thrive on love and attention and I've tried to help supply them. Now, with the center closed and their mothers having to return to work soon, I'm afraid they won't get that feeling of security so necessary for children, especially in circumstances like this."

She went on to voice more of her concerns.

There was something about her story that caught his interest: the importance of nurturing to a child's healthy development, mental as well as physical. Human development was his field, too, although his research had shown him genetic inheritance was just as important as a nurturing environment. Perhaps even more so.

He had to concede there was some evidence children needed a rich early life. But he was willing to bet her statement was based on opinion—hardly scientifically valid. His understanding of the subject was the result of years of scientific research. He settled down to listen more closely.

The woman was tall and slender. Dressed in jeans and a pullover sweater that accentuated all the womanly places on her anatomy, Miss Walker looked more like a schoolgirl herself than a schoolmarm. Surprise of surprises, her fresh face caught his eye, too. She wore no makeup, and her short auburn hair framed almond-shaped eyes, high cheekbones and a determined chin. She was definitely worth looking at.

What interested him even more than the school-marm, however, was the small boy who peeked around her legs. His hair hung over his wide eyes, and smiling lips were set in a small, round face. When the kid darted away from her to pick up a tiny puppy, Brady snapped to attention.

Where had he seen the child before?

There was something uncannily familiar in the shock of golden brown hair that kept falling over one eye, and the brilliant, mischievous smile as the boy gazed over this shoulder into the camera. Brady watched closely while the woman bent to affectionately stroke the boy's locks from his forehead. If the kid was hers, he sure hadn't inherited her coloring or any of her features.

They say everyone has a twin somewhere in the world who resembles him. If so, the child's father must have been Brady's twin. The boy certainly looked enough like Brady to be his son.

Brady's eyes swung to a small, framed snapshot that sat on the shelf behind him. It had been taken the first summer he'd spent with his aunt and uncle after his parents had set out on the first of a series of archaeological digs. Recognition flashed through him. His breath caught in his throat. Of course! What he was staring at was a copy of the snapshot his uncle had carried in his wallet for years. The young child in the picture was himself! And the boy on TV was a near duplicate of that child!

How could that be possible?

Shock waves ran through him as he turned back to watch the affectionate exchange on television between mother and son, before the camera moved on to show more of the damage at the day care. Unless he was badly mistaken, the boy on TV could have been him at that age. As if by magic, scenes from his childhood sprang into his mind. Icy fingers ran up and down his spine.

Somehow, from somewhere, Brady felt he knew the boy as well as he knew himself.

And he was going to find out how that could be.

WHAT A MESS! Jenny was down on her hands and knees, picking up wooden building blocks and putting them in an oversized laundry basket. Yet they were the least of her problems, she thought with a groan as she gazed around the room. Bookcases had come loose from the walls, tables and chairs were cracked and broken and tiles had fallen from the ceiling. Where was help when she needed it?

Suddenly a pair of running shoes came into her line of vision.

She heard someone clear his throat. Sinking back on her heels, she gazed upward until she encountered a man in a navy blue business suit, holding a briefcase. Running shoes and a business suit? Well, she thought as she suppressed a wry comment, the insurance company was certainly employing a nonconventional type.

She scrambled to her feet, dusted off her jeans and extended a welcoming hand. "Thank goodness you're here," she said with a sigh of relief. "Your office said it might take a while before you got around to inspecting the school. I can't tell you how grateful *I* am that you were able to come today." She gestured at the debris. "There's so much damage I don't know where to start to show you what's happened. But if you look around, I'm sure I don't have to explain much."

"You're right about that, Ms.—" he said, looking at her left hand.

"Jenny Walker," she answered with a slight frown as she followed his gaze. "I would have thought you'd have that information from your records. I'm the owner and operator of the school."

"Well, no, I don't have any of your records, but I am pleased to meet you. Actually, I saw you on television the other night."

"On television?" She frowned more deeply, then her face cleared. "Oh, right. But how did you find me?"

"They mentioned the school was in the San Fernando Valley. Besides, I could see the lopsided sign hanging over the door— Teddy Bear Care. How did you come up with a name like that?" He glanced around him for clues.

"Children love toys, and teddy bears are cuddly and comforting. Children relate to them," she answered, looking at him as if everyone should know that. "Didn't you have one when you were growing up?"

"No, can't say that I did." Toys? He couldn't remember more than one or two, and certainly not teddy bears. Mostly what he'd played with had been educational—chemistry sets, word puzzles and electronic equipment when it became available.

"That's too bad. You missed a lot." Genuine sympathy showed in her face as she turned her attention back to the room. "Well, now that you've seen the damage, you can get to work."

"Sure." He shifted his briefcase to his other hand and regarded the room. Derelict teddy bears, some worn building blocks and picture books were tossed helter-skelter as if by some giant hand. Kid-sized chairs and tables had fared no better. "It's sure a mess, isn't it?"

"Earthquakes have a way of doing that," she replied dryly. "That's why you're here, isn't it?"

"Sort of." He ignored the questions he saw forming in her eyes. "By the way, where are all the children you were talking about during the television interviews?"

"I don't see what that has to do with my insurance coverage, but if you need to know," she answered, frowning at him anew, "some are at home and a few are with my two aides at a neighboring church—that building was luckier than mine. The others are with relatives until this place is cleared up."

She waited for him to open his briefcase. "I'd like to talk about my insurance coverage, if you don't mind," she finally prompted when he made no move to get down to business. "What repairs are you prepared to authorize and how soon? I'm eager to get started so I can reopen."

"Sorry," he said, putting down his briefcase and focusing his attention on her. "I'm afraid you've misunderstood. I don't have your insurance policy."

"What kind of an insurance adjuster are you if you don't have a copy of my coverage?" Jenny eyed his briefcase suspiciously. The earthquake had brought all kinds of unsavory characters out of the woodwork, and this guy might be one of them. She'd had enough talk. She'd asked for help and she needed it now. He had to be reminded just what he was there for. "What do you carry in that?" she asked, gesturing to his case. "Your lunch?"

Just then a heavy aftershock shook the building. The floor heaved, throwing Jenny off-balance. Unable to steady herself, she stumbled on a wooden block and fell squarely in the arms that reached out to grab her.

BRADY CAUGHT his breath when he instinctively tightened his hold around the schoolmarm. Tall enough to fit squarely into his arms, she was soft where a woman should be soft and smelled as fresh as a spring morning. Her scent was of roses mingled with a faint spiciness. His gaze fastened on pink-tinged lips that were parted in shock, before moving back to her intriguing blue eyes. When their gazes locked, her exotic almond-shaped eyes seemed to deepen with wonder and, for a moment, something else.

He was shaken with an awareness he hadn't allowed himself to acknowledge for a long time. Buried deep in research for the past year, he hadn't taken the time to cultivate female relationships—or any other kind, for that matter. Yet this woman felt as if she belonged in his arms.

He was puzzled. If he'd known her from somewhere in time, surely he would have remembered. She looked to be the kind of woman no flesh-and-blood man would forget. And his response to her reminded him he certainly fit the description of red-blooded American male. He was surprised by the strong attraction he experienced during their chance embrace. And, unless he missed his guess, from the look in her eyes so was she.

Jenny Walker reminded him of what he'd been missing.

Trying hard not to display the near panic he felt, he held her in his arms while the building shook. The tremor reminded him of a dog shaking a bone. Books, toys and pictures that hadn't already fallen tumbled to the floor. Bits and pieces of plaster rained down from the ceiling.

Yet even as the building tottered, he wasn't so sure it was the aftershocks that were affecting him so strangely. Not while his heart pounded like a train arriving late at the station, and not while Jenny Walker clung to him as if her life depended on it.

"Are you all right?" he managed, belatedly realizing that she was struggling to get out of his arms. Reluctantly he let her go.

"Yeah, sure," she answered as she backed out of his embrace. Before she could regain her balance, another shock sent her back into his arms.

"Maybe you'd better let me hold you until this is all over," he said with a chuckle, clutching her to him as the ground shook anew. "No use inviting trouble."

"I could move if I wanted to," she replied, her teeth chattering as she clung to him with both hands.

The whisper of her breath against his neck sent his mind down paths better not traveled. At least not now, when a violent act of nature was going on. No gentleman would take advantage of her at a moment like this. It was one of the few times in his life he regretted the code of honor that had carried him this far. But under different circumstances, in a different time and place...

When the ground finally stopped moving, she glanced cautiously around and tried again to stand on her own. "Is it over?"

He laughed shakily. "Until the next shock, anyway. How are you doing?"

"I'm okay."

She straightened her clothing, ran her hands over her hips and glanced oddly at him before she looked away.

"Are you sure you're going to be all right?" he asked anxiously, a hand outstretched to catch her if the shaking should start again.

She tossed her head, and her complexion changed from white to rosy pink. "Good heavens, you must think I'm a fool. I apologize for acting like a child at a time like this. Especially since I don't even know your name!"

"You're no child, Ms. Walker," he assured her with a wry smile, instinctively reaching to touch her auburn hair. Strange, how he felt the need to touch her again. He let a few silken strands slide through his fingers. "Only human." *And very endearing in her distress.*

Jenny tried to pull herself together. Startled by her reaction to the man, she was chagrined to feel a warmth spreading through her middle. She'd been in his comforting arms for only a short time, but something had happened to her during those few seconds that had left her shaken and bewildered. And, she was afraid, not only from the aftershocks. She'd been through earthquakes before, but she'd never felt so warm and protected and so safe as now. She was also very aware of his striking masculinity.

Good heavens, she scolded herself, what was she thinking of? She didn't even know the man, let alone why she should have felt so secure and comforted in his arms. She'd never even laid eyes on him until a few minutes ago. There was no accounting for the response, unless it was because earthquakes were so unsettling.

"If you're not an insurance adjuster, just who *are* you?" she finally managed, aware she should have asked the question the first moment he'd walked in the door.

He smiled reassuringly. "My name is Brady Morgan. I'm writing a series of research papers on the effects of genetic inheritance versus environment with regard to child development. Your comments on TV interested me, even if I don't necessarily agree with you. I was hoping we could discuss your views."

Jenny sighed. Even if he'd practically saved her life, he was still a stranger, and a decidedly odd one at that. "Just what I needed—a scientific discussion at a time like this," she muttered as she eyed him cautiously. She reminded herself she had to be careful. "How do I know who you are? With the front doors off the hinges, anyone could come walking in here. Besides," she said, folding her arms across her suddenly tingling breasts, "how do I know if I can trust you?"

He looked at her under raised eyebrows. "I had a chance to have my way with you a few minutes ago, Ms. Walker, but I managed to contain myself, didn't I?" He couldn't tell her just how much she'd affected him, or that he hadn't wanted to let her out of his arms. Not if he expected her to allow him to hang around until he got the information he'd come for. He took a business card out of his inside breast pocket. "Maybe this will help to introduce me."

"'Dr. Brady Morgan, Thurgood Institute,'" she read aloud as she held the card at arm's length. *Drat, where had she put her reading glasses?* "I still don't know just what it is I can do for you, Dr. Morgan. Or, frankly, if I have the time for this conversation. I'm waiting for an insurance adjuster, and until he shows up I have a great deal of straightening up to do."

"I'll be glad to help," he volunteered with a winning smile. "We can talk while we work." He shrugged out of his jacket and rolled up his shirtsleeves. "Where do you want me to start?"

"Well, if you insist, I can sure use the help." She covertly checked to see that the path to the outside door was clear in case she decided to leave in a hurry. "How about helping me finish collecting building blocks before we straighten up?"

"Got it."

He pitched in immediately, helping her to gather the blocks before righting miniature tables and chairs. While she carried two at a time, four at a go seemed effortless in his large and capable hands. Warm, strong hands she could still feel holding her against the hard, masculine length of him.

Good heavens, she thought as she watched him right the upended wicker basket. What was there about the man that made her want to trust him? What had possessed her to let this stranger stay, when instinct told her she should have been exercising more caution? Still, how dangerous could a man who wore tennis shoes with a business suit be?

"Frankly, you made a few observations the other night that fit right in with a follow-up paper I'm writing," he said as he straightened the last pint-sized chair. When she looked dubious, he hurried to add, "If it's a question of compensation . . . ?"

When she frowned, Brady had the gut feeling that maybe he'd said the wrong thing. She obviously hadn't been asking for handouts. However, from what he'd heard during her TV interview, she was practically running a nonprofit institution, taking in children whose single mothers could barely afford to fully pay the small fee she charged. And often, as he understood it, taking in children free.

She wasn't in the child-care business for profit—that was obvious from the look of the place. And unless she had a great deal of earthquake insurance to cover the damage, the expenses for the repair might be a bigger blow than she realized. From what he'd seen and heard so far, she might even be forced to close the school.

"Perhaps you would consider a donation to help replace some of the things you've lost," he offered. "For the sake of the children you take care of, of course."

He watched with interest as she gazed around the room. She was obviously struggling with herself; her face grew more strained than before. Finally, her eyes darkened with emotion and her lips grew tight. She straightened her back and shook her head.

"Thank you, that's very thoughtful of you, but no. I was interviewed on television only because of the earthquake. I wasn't trying to solicit help. We'll manage somehow. It won't be the first time I've had to start over."

But hopefully, the last, if he had anything to do with it, Brady thought with a pang of compassion. She needed help and something moved him to want to supply it. Whatever her story, she was obviously a proud woman and used to fending for herself. As puzzling and intriguing as she had been on television, she was even more so now.

He felt a moment of guilt. What he was up to wasn't exactly fair to Jenny, but a man had to do what a man had to do. Even if it meant subterfuge.

It was the only way he could think of to legitimately see her again, to get her to talk to him. And not only for the sake of the boy who'd been with her during the television interview. He was drawn to this woman, no doubt about it. He glanced at her ring finger again. She called herself "Ms." Walker, but that didn't mean much. Most businesswomen today were Ms., married or not. Did she have a husband? Was the boy her son? And if not, who was his mother?

Somehow he needed to get the answers to those questions. And he sensed Jenny Walker was the only one who could tell him whether or not he was actually a father.

Chapter Two

Jenny eyed Brady cautiously as he picked up and dusted off a teddy bear and carefully placed it in a small chair. With his suit jacket off and shirtsleeves rolled up, he looked a little less odd than when she'd first laid eyes on him—but not by much. There *were* those tennis shoes.

He was a good six feet in height, and his lithe body telegraphed a lifetime of discipline. She'd bet he was the type who watched his calories and cholesterol and hadn't eaten a potato chip ever. His pale complexion told her he was an indoors man, which was strange. A build like his usually belonged to a guy who played tennis or enjoyed swimming. Brady what's-his-name looked as though he were a stranger to sunshine.

She tried to relax. The guy appeared to be harmless. She'd just spent a few highly charged minutes in his arms and everything had turned out okay, hadn't it? Except for her awakened hormones, which were still asking for relief.

She pulled his card out of her jeans pocket to refresh her memory. Brady Morgan was his name; of course.

She gazed at his golden brown hair, earnest brown eyes and the lopsided smile he was trading with the stitched smile on the teddy bear's face. A tender feeling washed over her.

Something told her he was a man she wasn't going to forget easily.

She tried not to be caught inspecting him, but the urge to tease him about his fascination with the bear was irresistible.

"So you like Alfred, do you? Is it because he reminds you of the teddy bear you had when you were little?"

"Alfred?" He turned his surprised gaze on her. "You mean you name your teddy bears?"

"Of course. It gives them a personality. Didn't you name yours?"

"Well, to tell you the truth I've never had one," he said.

That crooked, shy smile of his made her heart turn over. "What kind of toys *did* you play with?" Noting his hesitancy, Jenny went on, "Surely you did have toys."

"Actually," he answered, reaching to straighten Alfred, who was sliding off the chair, "my first toys were alphabet blocks and an electric typewriter. When I found out about computers, I lost interest in everything else. You might say I'm a computer junkie. Oh, yes, there were the piano and drums, but the drums went by the wayside when my folks enrolled me in boarding school."

"That's all?"

"Well, I still play the piano," he added with a grin, "but only when I need to relax."

"No *real* toys?" she asked. "How about games, playmates?"

"I'm not sure what you mean by real toys, but there were word games and other games of skill. And, of course, a few good friends. But no teddy bears."

"Weren't you *ever* a kid?" she gasped. He shrugged. "No wonder..." Her voice died away when she noticed his raised eyebrows. "Sorry, I didn't mean to cast any aspersions on your upbringing. It just seems to me children need to *be* children, to play and interact with other kids to develop healthy personalities."

After a moment's consideration, she realized she'd put her foot in it again. "Oh my goodness, I didn't mean to imply that you haven't had a healthy..." Impulsively she reached for Alfred and thrust him at Brady. "Here, take him. He's yours."

"It's a little too late for teddy bears, don't you think?" Brady laughed as he poked a stray bit of stuffing into Alfred's ear. "Not that I'm not grateful, you understand, but don't you think I'm too old for this kind of thing?"

"No," she answered firmly. "Take my word for it, you're never too old for tender, loving care, even the pretend kind from a stuffed animal. Teddy bears excel at making you feel good."

"Well," he said, gazing at her in way that made her feel all warm inside. "I never thought about it that way, but maybe you're right. Thank you.'' He walked over to where he'd left his briefcase and jacket and gently tucked Alfred into a pocket until only the bear's nose, eyes and the wounded ear were showing.

Another shock shook the building. Jenny started, eyes wide, and held her breath. She looked to Brady, ready to run for comfort. He smiled.

''That was just a three-pointer,'' he said. ''Mild, considering how strong the earlier ones were.''

''Yeah, but if you add them all up—'' she shivered ''—they're enough to unnerve anyone. Especially since they happen when you least expect them.''

''Want me to hold you, just in case?'' he asked, extending his arms.

''Absolutely not,'' she answered.

''Okay, now what?'' he said with one eye on the bear and the other on its former owner.

''You introduce yourself to Alfred,'' she said firmly. ''Yes, I know it sounds weird,'' she added as he started to protest, ''but it would help you bond with him.''

''Talk to a teddy bear?'' he repeated incredulously. ''That's about the last thing I'd care to be caught doing.''

''That's how you create the bond,'' she said reasonably. ''By talking to teddy bears, dolls and to people, for that matter.''

''I can understand the people part,'' he said. ''But teddy bears?''

''Sure. Every time we had one of those aftershocks and I was shook up, I found myself talking to Alfred or one of the other bears. Just sharing how uneasy I felt helped.'' *Until you came along to hold me.*

''I haven't been too happy about the shocks, either,'' he started as another tremor shook the building. ''Thank goodness I was in Denver when the quake hit. Where were you?''

''In bed, but not for long,'' she replied, poised to leave if things became any worse. ''I wound up in the street with the rest of the neighbors. These shakes haven't been easy to take, either. I've done a lot of talking to the bears in the past few days.''

He glanced around the room before he shrugged and looked back at the bear. ''Well, Alfred, if we're going to be roommates, I guess I should introduce myself. My name is Brady Morgan,'' he said with as straight a face as he could muster. ''I expect you're going to see a lot of me in the future.''

''That's a good start,'' Jenny said encouragingly, trying to hold back her laughter. ''It gets easier as time goes by.''

''Maybe. What's next?'' he asked, sending Alfred an apologetic glance. He'd be darned if he was going to be caught talking to a stuffed animal when there was a decidedly more interesting person available.

Touched by his genuine embarrassment, Jenny cleared her throat. She was determined to get off personal matters and back to business before she lost the rest of her good sense.

''We pick up all the papers and crayons and clean up the spilled paint. Thank goodness the paint is water based," she said as she ruefully regarded the streaks of red, green and yellow paint on the wooden floors, "but it's still a devil to get rid of entirely. Well, I can wash the floors later. Right now let's get back to straightening up."

"I'd be happy to take care of the paint for you."

"I'm sure you could, but not in those white tennis shoes," she answered, gesturing at his feet. Curiosity got the better of her. "If you don't mind my asking, why tennis shoes? They look out of character. They certainly don't go with the rest of your outfit."

"I don't mind at all. After the way things around here appeared on television, I didn't want to break an ankle stepping on loose bricks."

"Smart thinking," Jenny conceded. A thought occurred to her. "Say, do you plan everything you do so carefully?"

"Everything," he replied after a short, meaningful pause. His smile came and went before she had a chance to decide if he was talking about tennis shoes or something else.

One thing was certain: she wasn't sure she was ready for the way he eyed her from her head to her toes.

"The brooms are in the closet at the back of the room, if you still want to help," she said firmly, leading the way. "First things first." She gasped and reached for something to hold on to as another aftershock tilted the floor under her feet.

Tables and chairs that had recently been righted toppled on their sides with a series of crashes. The basket holding the wooden blocks slid across the room and into the last upright bookcase. Storybooks rained down on the floor. The small radio she'd brought from home so she could keep up with the news fell to the floor with a squawk. A rubber ball bounced across the room and caught her in the pit of her stomach. Taken by surprise, she staggered backward.

And found herself in Brady Morgan's arms.

Maybe this was meant to be, Brady thought as he pulled her close and savored the heady feel of holding her. He'd been right the first time; she did belong in his arms. When she turned around and buried her face in his shirt, he had to smile. He gave her a reassuring squeeze. Maybe Someone up there was telling him something. On second thought, considering the gravity of the situation, maybe he was enjoying the moment too much.

Jenny was too great a distraction. He had to pull himself together and concentrate on—as she herself had said—"first things first." And in his game plan, the boy definitely came first.

He swallowed his smile when he felt her tremble and burrow closer into his chest. The urge to comfort her, to keep her safe, came over him. He glanced down at her sweet-smelling auburn hair with something more than sympathy.

One thing was sure: from what she'd said a few minutes ago, Jenny Walker needed a big dose of the tender, loving care of the human kind. And he was ready, willing and able to supply it.

Moved by compassion, he did something he never would have dreamed of doing under any other circumstances, especially with a woman he'd just met. But this was a major crisis if ever there was one. With a gentle hand, he lifted her chin until her startled eyes met his. Slowly, carefully, he bent his head and brushed her lips with his own. The warmth of her lips, the cinnamon and honey taste of her, was more than he'd bargained for.

Easy, he told himself as he looked into her exotic blue eyes, *the lady is vulnerable now.* Reluctantly he ended the light kiss before it became something more. Her eyes locked with his, and a becoming blush came over her cheeks. Whatever he'd felt, it appeared that she shared the feeling.

What had come over him? He had meant only to comfort her, to give her a dose of the tender, loving care she so obviously needed, not make love to her. Whatever his intention originally, it seemed that they were both shaken by his unexpected reaction to the kiss.

"I'm sorry," he said as she moved out of his arms. "I don't know why I did that. Maybe I ought to leave before things get out of hand. That is, if you think you'll be okay alone."

"Maybe you should," she agreed, looking everywhere but into his eyes. "The insurance adjuster will be here soon. I wouldn't want him to get the wrong impression of what's going on."

Brady reached for his coat and met Alfred's accusing eyes. The bear was right, and so was she. Things *were* getting out of hand. Time to retreat from the field while he still had his honor, he told himself. Remembering what he'd come for, he paused. "By the way, there was something I wanted to check out. The boy who was with you on television. Is he your son?"

"Why, yes." She was surprised at the question. "Why do you want to know?"

"I was just struck by the display of affection between the two of you during the interview."

"That's what mothers are for," she said as she handed him his briefcase.

Brady shrugged. "I wouldn't know. I was raised in boarding schools, with nary a mother or a teddy bear in sight." He put on his jacket, careful not to disturb the watchful Alfred. He could already tell the bear was destined to be his conscience. He felt an overwhelming need to see Jenny Walker again, to talk to her, to see her son. To find out why the boy looked so familiar. Casually he put a hand over Alfred's eyes; he didn't need the bear's opinion.

"By the way, when you have time I would still like to discuss a few of your theories about personality development." When he saw the doubt rise in her eyes, he hurried to add, "For the sake of research, of course."

"I'm not sure what kind of contribution I could make," Jenny said, thinking about how quickly a relationship seemed to be developing. And wondering if it was wise to let it continue. The appeal of Brady's crooked smile decided the issue. She would like to see him again, if only she could pick a neutral place and stay out of arm's reach. What could possibly happen during a scientific discussion?

"Come back in a few weeks when things are a little more normal. We can talk then."

He nodded, saluted her and, with the smile that had already ensnared her, headed for the open doors. He stopped in front of a bulletin board outside her office, which was covered with photos of the school's children.

"This is your son, isn't it?" he said, pointing to a photo. "Handsome boy. How old is he?"

"Yes, he's my son," she replied with a soft smile as she came up behind Brady. "That's my Max. He's four."

IF THE SMILING LITTLE BOY in the photo resembled anyone, it had to be his father, Brady reflected as he drove home. Jenny Walker and the boy looked as completely different as they possibly could.

But heck, if he'd ever made love to Jenny, he sure would have remembered. Maybe he wasn't the boy's father.

As he pondered the thought, mental light bulbs suddenly came on. The answer was so obvious he could have kicked himself for being so dense.

Until this moment, mere curiosity had brought him to the school. Now, as he recalled gazing at the photos, he realized what must have been hidden at the back of his mind all along.

He recalled participating in a program started by the institute. Four years or so ago, he'd been approached to donate to the sperm bank it operated. He'd been told its goal was to give babies the best possible start in life through having fathers of high intelligence. Only when Brady's research brought him to the conclusion that genetic inheritance played a major role in human development had he reluctantly agreed.

Challenged by the appeal to his scientist's instincts, he'd gone through with the donation. When told he would never see the recipient or any child as a result of his contribution, he'd forgotten all about it.

Until now.

His reaction to the photo confused him. His first instinct was a distant one. Who needed fatherhood anyway? He'd gotten this far without it; his absorbing research took all his attention and his single, free lifestyle suited him just fine. He called his own shots. His life was his own.

Besides, from what he'd seen, being a father was a big responsibility. At least it would be for him. No child of his would grow up in boarding schools as he had. Being the type of father he would want to be wouldn't leave him much time for the research that fascinated him. Perhaps it was just as well that he hadn't married and fathered a child.

On second thought, when he contemplated it, he felt a faint stirring of an emotion he'd never felt before. Because of his sperm donation, maybe he did have a child. Maybe even a son. Maybe, he pondered with mixed emotions, the child was Ms. Walker's Max.

He thought about the photograph on the bulletin board with renewed interest. Would his son also have an unruly shock of hair that continually fell across his forehead into his eyes? Would it be the same as the one that fell over Max's eyes? Would his son's eyes be brown and sparkle with the same kind of humor as in the photograph that had drawn him? Would the boy have inherited his general build or his IQ? Had he inherited his love of science? His passion for music? If so, what instrument would he have picked?

And what about the child's mother? he wondered as his thoughts took a logical direction. Was she a good mother? Did she have the extraordinary patience it took to raise an intelligent child? What were her circumstances? He knew she had had to answer the same type of lengthy questionnaire he'd struggled over for days. She would have had to be healthy, to have a good biological family history of her own. And her personality traits would have had to be excellent for her to have been considered for motherhood, her desire for a child more than a whim.

More to the point, was his son happy? Did he have the toys and friends Jenny Walker maintained were necessary for a child's healthy mental development?

The longer Brady thought about the photograph, the more he realized how much small Max fit the description he envisioned for his own child. In an unconscious gesture, he pushed his hair away from his forehead.

Again it hit him—he and the boy looked enough alike to be father and son!

"REMEMBER THAT sperm donation you talked me into about five years ago?"

Haunted by the idea that Max might actually be his son, Brady had called Doug Cooper, his friend at the sperm bank, when he returned to his apartment.

"Heck, I'm so busy here I don't remember yesterday, let alone five years ago! You have no idea of the lineup of women we have who want to become mothers. We're doing our best to accommodate them. Say, do you want to donate again?"

"No, thanks." Brady laughed. "That's not why I called."

"So, what's up?"

"I was wondering if you knew whether my donation was used."

"What?" Doug's disbelief came through loud and clear. "You've got to be kidding! Any donation made five years ago is bound to have been used by now. What makes you ask?"

"Never mind." Brady thought rapidly. He *had* to know, but he was reluctant to give any details. "Is there any way you can find out for sure?"

"No way! The next thing I know you're going to want to find out who it went to. Right?"

"Right." Brady held his breath as he waited for the answer. He was so close to uncovering the truth, and yet so far.

"Wrong! Come on, you've been around long enough to know I've been sworn to secrecy. You signed a statement agreeing not to find the recipient of the sperm. You even gave up any claim to the child, if there was one. No, sir! I don't care how good a friend you are. That information is never revealed. Not under any circumstances!"

"You're right. Sorry, buddy, I shouldn't have asked. Talk to you later."

Brady hung up before Doug could ask questions. Even if he couldn't get an official answer, he'd find out the truth somehow. He couldn't give up. Not now. He thought for a few minutes. First things first, as Jenny Walker would say, he remembered with a smile. He'd invite himself over to his uncle's house, ask to look at the snapshot and see if his memory was on target.

JENNY SANK onto the floor and regarded the remaining teddy bears, which Brady Morgan had meticulously arranged in a row before he left.

"Well, Matilda, what do you think of that?" she asked a teddy bear who wore a skirt and had ribbons behind each ear. "The guy shows up out of nowhere and wants to know my views on raising children. Crazy, huh?" The wide-eyed bear quietly returned her gaze.

"You're right, of course," Jenny added. "There's something more here than meets the eye, isn't there? But whatever it is, I'm taking him far too seriously. He's just someone passing through. Between you and me, though—" she bent to whisper in Matilda's ear "—I kind of liked it when he held me in his arms.'' Jenny got to her feet and gazed down at Matilda. ''But the man does needs to lighten up a little. That's why I sent Alfred home with him.'' *Too bad,* Jenny thought as she gathered her things, waved goodbye and made ready to leave. Under different circumstances, Brady Morgan would have been fun to reform.

''WELL, BRADY, glad to see you're able to tear yourself away from your research long enough to remember I'm still alive. Haven't seen you in months. Come in the den and tell me why you're here.'' Ted Morgan led the way to the bookcase-lined room and gestured to a worn leather chair. ''Have a seat. Coffee?''

''Yes, thanks. Make it black.'' Brady laughed and sank into the oversized chair. ''Ted, you know me too well. What makes you think I want something? Maybe I just needed to touch base with my only uncle. You *are* my family.''

''True,'' Ted answered, handing Brady a steaming cup of coffee and going back to pour one for himself. ''Usually the only family you seem to be interested in are the ones in those scientific journals of yours.''

Brady sighed. Ted, as he'd called his uncle since adulthood, was being brutally frank. Brady knew he had it coming. He studied his uncle, a man he loved as a father. He was tall and spare, with a full head of graying hair and brown eyes that shone with affection. A noted psychologist, he'd retired to a life of writing, his latest book was on the *New York Times* bestsellers list. But as busy as he was, he was always ready to spend time with Brady.

"I'm just beginning to realize that I haven't done much besides research," Brady agreed, thinking of Jenny Walker. "But lately things have changed."

"Great!" Ted sat down in a matching chair, leaned back and crossed his legs, and eyed him with interest. "Finally met the woman of your dreams, did you?"

"Good Lord!" Brady choked on his coffee. How had his uncle guessed what had been going through his mind? "What makes you say that?"

"For what other reason would a man like you start thinking about visiting his only relative? In my experience, when a man meets a woman he wants to marry his thoughts turn to connecting with his own family. Am I right?"

Brady carefully placed his cup on the coffee table. In one corner of its scarred surface, he could see his name in block letters. He had managed to engrave it on the wooden surface when his uncle had first taught him how to print. At the time, Brady had been at least a year or more younger than Jenny's son, Max.

"No. Not even close." He grinned sheepishly at his uncle, too embarrassed to tell him what had been floating through his mind. "I haven't even had the time to look around."

"So what brings you here tonight?"

"To tell you the truth, I suddenly remembered the snapshot you carry in your wallet. The one of me, Mom and Dad. Could I look at it?"

"That's a strange request, but sure." Ted Morgan reached in his pocket for his wallet, opened it and handed over the snapshot. "I assume there's a story behind the need to see this tonight. Am I right?"

Brady studied the worn snapshot. Taken when he was around four or five, it was the color snapshot he'd remembered. Light-brown hair fell over one side of his forehead, bright brown eyes sparkled with humor. Even the impish smile was the same. He had been right: the young face in the photo could have been Max's.

Out of habit, he pushed his hair away from his forehead—the stray lock that had bedeviled him all his life. It had become his trademark. And Max had it, too.

"Brady? Are you all right?"

He heard his uncle's voice as if from a distance. All right? He was as all right as any man could be when confronted with an unknown son for the first time.

"Brady!"

The alarm in his uncle's voice shocked him out of his reverie. "I'm fine, really." He pulled himself together, handed the snapshot back to his uncle. Emotionally drained, he sank back in his chair. "That is, I will be in a minute."

"Are you sure?" Ted put his hand on Brady's knee and searched Brady's face. "You look as if you've seen a ghost!"

"I guess you could say that." Brady waited until his heart settled down to a normal beat. "Can you tell me what you remember about me before I was sent away to boarding school?"

Ted cursed softly. "You should never have been sent away. You changed so much it still bothers me to think about it."

"I recall being a pretty happy-go-lucky kid," Brady prompted, thinking of Jenny Walker's similar reaction at the mention of boarding school. *Had he missed something and not even been aware of it?* "If I changed, became more serious, it must have been in college. What do you remember about me?"

"You were seven when they sent you away. And until then a happy, normal boy, even if you were brighter than most. And the most inquisitive kid I've ever met. I told my brother he was overreacting to the intelligence test they had you take when it was obvious you were smarter than the rest of us. Up to that time, you had private tutors and me to teach you. You were so smart it became a game to see how much you could learn." A hint of tears came into Ted's eyes. "I blame myself for allowing it."

"Come on, learning new things was a game to me, too," Brady assured him. "I liked school, and besides, I had you and Aunt Ellie to come home to on holidays. I didn't turn out too badly, did I?"

"Not at all," Ted answered. "But you're so bound up in your work you haven't taken the time to enjoy yourself."

"I do in my own way," Brady reassured him. "You have nothing to be sorry for."

"You're too damn serious for a young man your age, Brady. Hell, you're only thirty-two!" Ted wiped his eyes with the back of his hand and smiled ruefully. "It's time for you to look around and smell the roses. Find a wife and have some children, for Pete's sake. Just because your Aunt Ellie and I couldn't have children, there's no reason for you to land up alone like me."

"Maybe I already have a child," Brady said softly.

"You what?" Ted shot out of his chair. "You *maybe* have a child?"

"A son."

"How can you maybe have a son? Either you do or you don't." Ted Morgan took the snapshot out of Brady's hand. "Does this have anything to do with it?"

"In a way." Brady smiled reassuringly. "Give me a few minutes and I'll tell you all about it." He went on to explain about his sperm donation and how he'd discovered Max on TV.

"Good God!" Ted studied the snapshot as if he were seeing it for the first time. "What are you going to do about the boy?"

"I'm not sure yet, but I'm not going to ignore him. I have to learn the truth." Just being able to talk about Max was a relief. It was as though he'd come to a crossroads in his life. Which road to take became clear even as he contemplated his choices.

"Brady, my boy, listen to me."

Obviously distressed, his uncle paced the floor.

"I hope you don't plan on doing anything foolish. These are people's lives you're playing around with. The boy may already have a father. Just because yours doesn't act like one doesn't mean every man acts that way.''

Ted was right. Brady's parents were archaeologists who spent their lives traveling through the Old World and living in the past. If any man was his father, it was his uncle.

Brady swore he was going to be different. He had to pursue finding out the truth. If Max was his son, he couldn't walk away from him. Never.

''You're right, Ted. It isn't going to be easy, especially if Ms. Walker proves difficult, but I'll be damned if I let much more time go by without getting to know my son.''

Chapter Three

Eighteen pairs of solemn young eyes regarded Brady from the large rug spread on the nursery-school floor. The nineteenth pair, framed by auburn hair that flowed around a smiling face, belonged, thank heavens, to a decidedly more mature grown-up; Jenny Walker. In the center of the rug, chin resting on his hand, sat Max. The boy's inquisitive eyes met his. Brady nodded a tentative hello, all the while keeping a cautious eye on the children. There were more small bodies in one place than he'd ever encountered before. Their silent scrutiny unnerved him.

"You're a little early, Mr. Morgan," Jenny said when she noticed him. "Maggie," she called to a young teenager who was collecting building blocks and putting them in a basket, "can you finish reading the story while I speak to our visitor?" She motioned to Brady to wait at the door.

Clad in blue jeans and a beige pullover sweater covered with white, fuzzy teddy bears, Jenny Walker didn't look much older than her teenager helper, Brady thought. Her hair was caught high at the back of her head in a ponytail that bounced with every step she took. The hair gadget that held the ponytail in place was the same color as her sapphire blue eyes. Whimsical blue-rimmed reading glasses were perched on her nose. Small gold earrings sparkled in her ears. A smile teased her lips as she turned her gaze from the children to him.

Her slim hips were definitely womanly, he noted with interest as she rose from where she sat cross-legged on the rug. She was no mere teenager, no matter how she might appear at a glance. And, all in all, as a total feminine package, Jenny looked more womanly than any other woman of his acquaintance.

What was he doing? he wondered as she made her way toward him. He should have been focusing on Max; instead his thoughts were thoroughly diverted by the boy's mother.

"Story hour is still going on," she whispered as she joined him. "Most of the children aren't picked up before six."

"That's okay," Brady replied, "I'll just wait back in the corner until you're ready."

Glancing over his shoulder at the open door, she frowned. "How did you get in anyway? I have an assistant who should have stopped you."

"I rang the doorbell. When no one answered, I tried the door. It was open, so I just walked in."

"So much for my other assistant, Cindy, and the guaranteed repair job to the door," Jenny muttered.

"This is supposed to be a secure building, with restricted entry. The way it appears, anyone could get in."

"I can take a look at the door while I'm waiting," Brady said, trading watchful glances with the children.

"You?" She stared doubtfully at his dark-blue business suit, white shirt and paisley tie. "And what do you plan on doing after you take a look?"

Taken aback by her question, Brady quickly inventoried his apparel. He had to concede he didn't resemble a carpenter. But, given the chance, he'd show her clothes didn't make or break the man they covered. "I'm going to try to fix it. I may not look like it, but I can handle a mean hammer."

"Maybe later," she replied, taking a sidelong glance at his feet as she turned back to the children. Now sensibly shod in sturdy brogues, Brady felt totally respectable and ready for anything. When she nodded, he knew he'd passed some kind of a test.

He headed for the teddy-bear brigade strewn on the floor at the back of the room. One by one he picked up the bears and arranged them neatly side by side in a row of small chairs. Maybe he should have brought Alfred with him, he thought, in high humor now that it appeared that he'd been accepted. The bear would probably have enjoyed a reunion with his friends.

Two weeks ago he hadn't even thought about stuffed animals. Now, he admitted with a smile of satisfaction, he'd found himself talking to Alfred on more than one occasion. Of course, the bear couldn't hear him, let alone respond, but it sure helped being able to voice his thoughts.

They'd discussed, in a one-sided conversation, Brady's possible fatherhood and all its ramifications. Alfred hadn't looked convinced, but then, Jenny Walker was the bear's mother, sort of, so Alfred had to see to her interests. Brady laughed silently as he tried to fit his tall frame onto a small chair. He was thinking of teddy bears as if they were human!

When his knees nearly touched his chin, he put his arms around them to keep himself from toppling over. Feeling like a pretzel, he glanced at his watch. There was still a half hour to go.

He glanced around the room while he was waiting. It seemed as if enough repairs had taken place in the past two weeks to allow Jenny to reopen, but the place still looked as though a hurricane had swept through it.

Aside from the few derelict teddy bears, worn building blocks, picture books and sundry toys, the room was bare. If there had been much more destruction, the school probably would have been damaged beyond repair. Large butcher-paper drawings done by the children were the only bright addition to the room since he'd been there two weeks ago.

He would have to try again to get Jenny to take a donation, he decided. She sure could use a little help to replace the toys damaged in the quake and maybe purchase some new play equipment for the schoolyard he'd seen in back of the building. He made a mental note to buy a few toys and bring them with him the next time he came over, or maybe... He straightened up in his enthusiasm and nearly toppled off the chair.

He'd take mother and son on a shopping expedition! Jenny Walker might be able to say no to him, but he doubted she could resist if Max wanted something.

He glanced over at the boy. The rest of the children were listening to the story, but not Max. When their eyes met, a wide grin spread over Max's face. The grin was so infectious that Brady found himself grinning back. Looking at Max was like looking into a mirror. As far as he could see, the resemblance between the boy and him was even greater in person than in the snapshot or the photo on the bulletin board.

A strong feeling of kinship with the little boy swept over him. If it turned out as he suspected and he was Max's father, he intended to *be* a father. Not that he knew how, but by God, he intended to learn. There were going to be shopping trips, trips to the zoo, even Disneyland, heaven help him! He planned on being around the boy and his mother as often as he could. When he met Max's bright eyes, he felt the time couldn't come too soon.

Was Max able to read his thoughts? If so, did the sparkle in the boy's eyes mean he was ready, willing and able to aid and abet Brady in the shopping trip he had in mind? What kind of toys would Max be interested in? If he was anything like Brady, he would want a computer with a CD-ROM. And a scanner. If they had been available when Brady was a kid, they were the type of things he would have chosen. Maybe a visit to a computer store would be in order after he bought some conventional toys. Maybe he'd even purchase a simple computer for the schoolroom!

He wondered how to ask Jenny about the boy's birth. As for finding out if he was the boy's father, that was touchy. How did a man go about asking a woman if she had been artificially inseminated in order to become a mother? And how to suggest that he might have been the donor? He hadn't come up with the answers, but he was working on it.

On the other hand, if it turned out Max wasn't his son, and if he *did* have a son somewhere, he would want him to be just like Max.

He turned his attention back to Jenny, who was again reading to the children. In no time, he was caught up in the story of Curious George, a monkey who was evidently so curious he got himself in and out of trouble all the time. From the children's delighted laughter, George was a favorite character.

The story held him enthralled, as well. If stories like this had been around when he was this young, he didn't remember having heard them. Maybe Jenny and his uncle were right: he had missed a lot. As for Jenny Walker, well, she could have been reading a laundry list and he'd still be interested.

Enchanted again by Jenny's animated voice, warm smile and enthusiasm for the story she was reading, he was struck by what an interesting woman she was.

First teddy bears, he mused, now monkeys; both creatures with human traits. It was obvious Ms. Walker was a woman who loved children and animals and worried over the emotional development of strays like himself. And from the way the children obviously adored her, she must deal out large doses of tender, loving care along with teaching them their letters and numbers and how to get along with one another.

The more he watched and listened, the more he became impressed with the woman as well as the teacher. He thought of his instinctive reaction to the light kiss they'd exchanged. Imagined what it would be like to have her soft and warm in his arms without an aftershock having sent her there.

Propelled by Jenny's magic, he realized he was thinking irrationally for the first time in his life. What if she had a husband or a significant other? He needed to find out.

READING AUTOMATICALLY, Jenny felt her mind wander from the antics of Curious George and to the man who displayed such an avid interest in the story. Now that she was seeing him again, she had the strangest feeling she knew him from someplace. Yet where? She couldn't recall, but it must have been a long time ago or she would have remembered.

She had to fight to keep from breaking into laughter as she saw him try to get comfortable. Almost six feet too tall for the pint-sized chair, he wasn't going to be able to manage that miracle no matter how hard he tried. To make things more ludicrous, he'd aligned himself alongside the teddy bears, as if one of them.

There were Reuben, Jane, the Cisco Kid and Matilda—stuffed animals all—and Brady Morgan, the weird scientist, all silently regarding her.

"All right, children," she said as she came to the end of the story and closed the book. "Make sure you have your jackets and backpacks and come line up by the door."

A young woman rushed into the room. "Gee, I'm sorry, Jenny. I was out back picking up tricycles and putting the sand toys away, when I looked in the window and saw this man here. I didn't let him in. Did you?"

She gazed at Brady suspiciously. He rose to his feet, as if ready to defend his right to be there.

"No, I didn't, but it's okay." Jenny waved the girl off and eyed Brady with amusement. "We'll talk about it later, Cindy. In the meantime, go stand by the door and check off whoever arrives to pick up the kids. Make sure everyone signs out."

Breathless, her assistant nodded, grabbed a clipboard and disappeared into the hallway.

Max wandered up to Brady. "Hi," he said, checking Brady up and down. "Whose Daddy are you?"

Brady's heart skipped as he gazed down at the piquant face of the boy who—in his own mind, at least—was fast becoming his son. Knowing that stray lock would only fall back again, he restrained himself from reaching out and pushing it out of the boy's warm and trusting eyes. He'd forgotten, if he'd ever known, just how trusting and candid children could be. But, until he was positive the boy was his child, he wasn't going to take advantage of that trust.

"My name is Brady Morgan. I'm just visiting for now."

Brady was prepared to shake hands. Max apparently wasn't having any of him.

"And who are you?" Brady inquired.

"Can't tell you," Max said. "My mommy said never to tell anyone my name or where I live. No matter what."

"Your mother is right," Brady replied solemnly. "No matter what."

"And what are you two having such a serious discussion about?" Jenny asked as she finally joined them.

"How to stay out of trouble," Brady said with as straight a face as he could manage. "You've trained your son well. He won't even give me his name."

"Of course not. But—" she turned to Max "—it's okay now that I'm here. Mr. Morgan is doing some research and is going to spend some time talking about it with me tonight."

"Okay, Mom," the boy agreed. "If you say so. My name is Max Pullman Walker, Mr. Morgan."

"Great, Max." Brady offered his hand again. This time the boy returned the handshake. The small hand, warm in his large one, sent a wave of emotion through Brady. He felt tender, protective. He didn't remember ever having felt this way before. He gazed down into brown eyes bordering on amber, so like his own. Was this his son? He swallowed the hard lump in his throat.

He had to take things easy, one step at a time. "What do you say if I treat you and your mother to dinner?"

"It's McDonald's night, Mr. Morgan," Jenny explained with a laugh. "We go there every Wednesday when they have a Happy Meal special and children's movies. You might want to take back your offer."

"Not at all," he responded as he noted Max's anxious eyes. "I'd be delighted to have a Happy Meal." The genuine smile that came over Max's face brought a smile to his own heart.

"Then thank you. We'd enjoy taking you up on your invitation, wouldn't we, Max?"

Max nodded and tugged at Brady's trousers. "You don't have to order a Happy Meal, Mr. Morgan. That's for us kids. They have grown-up hamburgers, too."

"In that case, you're definitely on. Just point out the direction and we'll go. I'll drive."

"You don't know what you're getting into, Mr. Morgan," Jenny whispered as Max scampered off to get his jacket. "The place is full of children, and, I'm afraid, they're pretty noisy."

"Don't worry about it. I'm sure everything will turn out just fine. Anyway," he said, gazing wistfully after Max, "I guess it's time I became used to being around children."

JENNY WENT to get her coat and check on Cindy. His last remark told her a great deal about the man and answered questions she hadn't felt free to ask. He had no children, nor, if she missed her guess, had he ever been married. The meticulous way he'd lined up the tables, chairs, even teddy bears in perfect, neat little rows would have been enough to drive a wife crazy. Not to mention his having admitted to planning every step of his life.

She'd been married to someone like that once. Paul Walker had been an egocentric man whose plans had seldom included her, and never fatherhood. After five years, she'd given up trying to change him and had gotten a divorce. Until Max had arrived, the nursery school had been the answer to her longing to have children. Now she felt she had almost everything a woman could ask for.

She could tell she was as different from her visitor as day was from night. She was more the spontaneous, emotional type and loved being around people, especially children. From the wary look in Brady's eye as he watched the children's noisy leave-taking, she couldn't say the same for him. If she had ever entertained the thought of seeing Brady again, she dismissed it. Like oil and water, she and Brady Morgan would never mix.

What was she thinking of? she chided herself as she put on her coat and checked the room for a stray child. There would be dinner at McDonald's, an hour's worth of conversation and then she'd probably never see him again.

THE WAVE OF SOUND that greeted them as they came in the door of the popular fast-food restaurant made Brady cringe. It seemed as if there were dozens of children, all talking at once and drowning out the television set. He blinked at the pandemonium that filled the small restaurant and dutifully took his place in line along with Jenny. Max headed for his friends.

"Looks and sounds more like a football game than a restaurant," Brady laughed as two small children chased each other and darted into him. "No one is standing still long enough to eat!"

"You learn to tune out the noise after a while. It's kids' night out, after all."

Tray in hand, Brady grabbed a booth that was being vacated. "How do you find Max in all this?"

"He'll be back as soon as he gets hungry. That ought to take about ten minutes." She handed Brady his wrapped hamburger and soft drink. "Well, what do you think of all this, Mr. Morgan?"

"It is quite an experience, isn't it?" He unwrapped the hamburger and gazed incredulously at the two meat patties, tomatoes, pickles and dressing. There were more grams of fat in the one burger than he allowed himself in a week! As for calories, he shuddered to think about them. They might be all right for Max, who was still a growing bundle of energy, and maybe even for Jenny, but not for him. On second thought, those slim hips and narrow waist of hers weren't the product of untold calories.

He glanced around the crowded room. "Why don't you call me 'Brady'? There's no reason for formality. Especially in a place like this."

"Only if you call me 'Jenny,'" she replied with smile. "So tell me, how are you and Alfred getting along?"

"Great!" Brady paused. "As a matter of fact, I don't know how I managed this long without the bear to talk to. Which reminds me, Alfred needs an operation on his ear. Know where I can have it done?"

"Mom, can I take my Happy Meal and go eat with Tommy?" Max slid up to the booth. "His mother said it's all right with her if it's all right with you!"

"Sure, sweetheart. But come right back as soon as you're through." Jenny handed Max the decorated lunch bag. "And don't go anywhere else without me."

"Aw, Mom! And I promise not to talk to strangers, either, just like you said." With a teasing grin, he opened the bag and extracted the plastic toy that came with the meal. "Cool! I don't have this one yet!" With a parting grin, Max dashed away.

"He's some boy, isn't he?" Brady gazed admiringly across the room to where Max had found a seat. "Bright, too."

"Yes, he is. In fact, sometimes he scares me he's so bright."

"Didn't you know he would be?" Brady asked casually, biting into his hamburger. It was delicious and smelled as good as it tasted. Maybe, just for once, calories didn't count. He glanced over at Jenny who was unashamedly dipping French fries in catsup. If things continued to go so well, he might find out more about her son's conception without coming right out and asking.

"How can one predict how intelligent a child is going to be?" Jenny asked, looking puzzled. "Happily, Max is brighter than most children, but I didn't know he would be when I first saw him. But even if he wasn't, I'd love him just as much."

Impressed, Brady could only nod. Because he had never known such unconditional love himself, except from his aunt and uncle when he'd come home for vacations and holidays, Jenny's attitude made a deep impression on him.

"Now, just what was it you had on your mind?" Jenny moved the littered tray out of the way. "I'm afraid we'll have to leave soon. Tomorrow is a school day."

A burst of excited sound came from the vicinity of the television set. Max darted back to the table. "Mom, Tommy wants me to sleep over at his house tonight, Can I?"

"Not tonight, sweetheart. There's school tomorrow." She leaned over and wiped a smear of catsup from Max's cheek. "I'll phone his mother and we'll make it for another time."

"Aw, Mom. I want to go!"

"Not tonight," she repeated firmly. "Now, go and play. I'll call you when it's time to leave."

Inwardly shuddering at the noise around him, Brady struggled to appear nonchalant. This was no place to conduct a serious conversation, even if he wanted to. And he didn't want to, not if it meant he wouldn't have a reason to see Jenny and her son again.

What had started out as an interest in the differences between nature and nurture to the human psyche had turned into a search for his son. He'd have to get around to discussing it with Jenny sooner or later, the sooner the better. Anything else came second. He couldn't give up now.

He felt a momentary pang of guilt for using Jenny Walker. Not that he wanted to take the boy away from her if it turned out he was his son. She was a good mother and Max seemed to have thrived under her tender, loving care. He just wanted to see Max regularly, perhaps even share him—if she'd let him.

"Tell you what," he finally offered. "There's plenty of time to talk later. I'll come over to the school Saturday afternoon and have a look at the door. It's probably just out of alignment. I'm sure it'll close properly once that's taken care of."

"Okay. Maybe you're right." She gazed at Brady thoughtfully. The man was a bundle of contradictions. "Where did you learn carpentry? Surely not at the boarding school you described."

"My uncle and I made a few things together during the summers. He told me a man needs to know how to do simple repairs. That included how to change a light bulb," Brady offered with a crooked grin.

"Sorry, the light bulbs at the school are all working just fine," Jenny said playfully. "Oh, and by the way, bring Alfred along with you—I'll sew up his ear. You see, my mother taught me it was vital for a woman to learn how to do simple repairs, too."

"It's a deal. I'll be there Saturday with Alfred," Brady agreed as they traded amused glances. What was wrong with him? He was here to meet Max, and all he could think of was seeing Jenny again. Astonished at the direction his thoughts were taking, he hesitated only a moment before he plunged in. He wanted to see Jenny somewhere quiet, to have her all to himself. The school, with its small audience, wasn't the place he envisioned.

"Frankly, that's not what I had in mind for our discussion," he corrected. "I'd like to take you out to dinner tomorrow night." He sat back in his seat and watched as a surprised look came over her face.

"You want to take me out to dinner?" Jenny repeated. "Why would you want to do that? We hardly know each other!"

"True, but the best way to get to know someone is through sharing a meal and conversation. Right?"

Jenny's reaction to the man didn't make much sense to her, but she found herself more than willing to agree with him. Maybe it was the expression on his face that drew her. It reminded her of Max when he wanted something special and was afraid she wouldn't say yes.

Or maybe Brady was more than he seemed. Maybe, she thought as she studied him, she shouldn't have written him off as being so different from herself and probably difficult to get along with. After all, weren't scientists supposed to be pragmatic? And what if he *was* too meticulous? Nobody was perfect. If he hung around Max and the nursery school long enough, they'd soon lighten him up. She knew from experience that children had a way of keeping you from taking yourself seriously.

"You're on. That is, if I can find a baby-sitter for Max," she answered, smiling at his relieved expression. Yes, she thought, he *was* a lot like a kid who was afraid he wouldn't get what he wanted. And was happy when he did. "Maybe Cindy will come over for a few hours."

"I'll pick you up." He reached for a clean paper napkin, then took his pen from his breast pocket. "What's your address?"

"I thought we came here to exchange views on children," Jenny said, eyeing the napkin. "Didn't you bring a notebook to take notes?"

"Well, no," Brady replied, pen poised. "I guess you could say I have a photographic memory and near-perfect recall of what I hear. I usually don't need written notes. Right now, I figure it's the noise in here that's turning me off."

"If you say so." She gave him the address to her place and directions. "Now, where do you suppose Max has gone off to?" Glancing around the crowded room, she frowned when she couldn't see him and started to rise. Brady put his hand on hers.

"I think I just saw him head out the door to the play area. I'll get him and we'll be back in a minute."

Through the glass door, Brady had seen Max hanging upside down on the jungle gym. He didn't have the experience to know for certain, but it looked like the wrong position for a kid to be in right after he'd eaten a cheeseburger and fries. His own stomach rebelled at the thought.

"Come on, fella," Brady said as he supported Max's wiggling hips and lifted him off the metal apparatus. "Your mother says it's time to go home."

"Aw, Mr. Morgan. Just five more minutes?"

"Sorry. We don't want to make your mother angry, do we?"

"Mom never gets mad at me," Max said, small white teeth flashing. "She just pretends to. She's the best!"

"You're probably right about that," Brady answered, glancing over his shoulder to where Jenny stood waving at the window. He waved back. "You're a lucky kid to have a mother-like her. But let's not take any chances."

Max reluctantly waved goodbye to his friends and put his hand in Brady's. "Okay, if you say so. But I really would like to stay."

"Another time. I promise to bring you back here again soon."

"Tomorrow?"

Max's radiant smile captured Brady's heart some more. He gently pushed the boy's hair out of his eyes. "No, I'm afraid not. Why don't we talk to your mother about that. Right now, I gather it's time to go home."

From the window, Jenny was intrigued by the strong resemblance between the two golden brown heads, as Brady bent over Max. And, when the two of them exchanged smiles, how the smiles were so similar. They were so much alike it was mind-boggling, even a little eerie.

Strange, too, how easy talking to Brady had become, how familiar. It had to be because anyone who resembled Max, her favorite person, was bound to catch her favor. Coincidence? she wondered, as she went to join them.

Chapter Four

The doorbell to her town house rang promptly at seven-thirty. Of course, Jenny mused as she adjusted a gold earring and took a last, hurried glance in the mirror. She should have known Brady would be on time.

When she reached the living room, Cindy, the baby-sitter, had already unlocked the door and let him in. Behind his back, she rolled her eyes and made an "A-OK" gesture with her fingers. Agreeing, Jenny winked.

Instead of the proper dark-blue business suit he'd worn the other day, Brady was dressed in beige chino slacks, a brown-and-blue checkered sport shirt open at the neck and a loose, brown linen jacket. Penny loafers were on his feet. Even his newly cut golden brown hair appeared stylish; the shock of hair that fell over one eye gave him a rakish look. The proper scientist was gone and a very cool nineties man had taken his place. No wonder Cindy was impressed.

Jenny quickly made a mental inventory of the ensemble she'd chosen to wear: a hunter green linen suit, maybe one inch too short, with a softly draped, white silk blouse. Compared with Brady, she felt over-dressed. The irony of it all was that she'd taken great care to dress up for him, while he'd lightened up for her! She studied him with dawning respect. There was obviously more than one side to Brady, and this was a side she was prepared to like.

"Hi, Mr. Morgan!" Max skipped into the room and skidded to a stop in front of Jenny. "Gosh, Mom, you look cool! Where are you going? Can Cindy and me come, too?"

"'Cindy and I,'" Jenny automatically corrected, "and no, you can't join us. We're going out for dinner and you've already eaten yours," she added firmly. "Your night out was at McDonald's. Tonight is for grown-ups."

"Aw, please, Mom?" When she shook her head, Max turned his wide brown eyes on Brady. "Can we come, too, Mr. Morgan?"

"Sorry, fella. Your mother is right. You're a little too young to qualify for dinner out tonight," Brady answered. His fingers itched to clear the boy's hair from his eyes. "Maybe we can take in McDonald's again next week."

"Now, Max," Jenny cautioned. "I meant what I said. I don't want to hear any more. Go upstairs and get ready for your bath. I'll take care of Mr. Morgan."

Brady felt sorry for the crestfallen boy, but after all, Brady wasn't a court of appeal, at least not yet. With a sympathetic eye he watched Max leave. Even at four—

maybe especially at four—"no" cut deep. "I'll have to take him to McDonald's again."

"You don't have to, you know." Jenny laughed. "Max is a great con artist. One wistful look with those big brown eyes of his and he usually gets what he wants."

"I want to take him," Brady replied with a smile as he glanced around him at the cozy French country living room and adjoining dining room. The contrast between Jenny's home and his own modern, strictly functional apartment was striking, even to him. Her place was a lot warmer, more inviting. It had a comfortable appeal that reminded him of his uncle's home, a home that had taken on the down-to-earth personality of its owner. As this one had taken on Jenny's. As for himself, he'd never felt the need for more than a place to eat, work and sleep; one that took a minimum of care.

As far as Brady could tell, there was no evidence anywhere of a male in residence, and still no ring on Jenny's finger. Cindy's presence confirmed that Jenny lived alone with Max. One of his questions had been answered. Jenny was either divorced or widowed; or, if she had never been married, she could have applied to a sperm bank to become the mother of Max. That it might have been *his* sperm that had produced Max became more and more possible.

Damn. He should just come out and ask her, but he hesitated. He was afraid her answer would erect a barrier between them, and he was interested in building bridges, instead.

"Nice place you have here," Brady finally remarked after tearing his gaze from hers. "Doesn't look as if the earthquake affected your home much, if at all."

"Thank you," Jenny replied, reaching for her coat. "We were lucky here. The only real damage was to the water heater and the bedroom walls upstairs, and they've been repaired. Oh, and some broken lamps, glass and dishes. How about you?"

"As I mentioned, I was in Denver when the quake happened. I came home to find my computer on the floor and some bookcases and shelves broken." He glanced around at the furnished room. "Happily, I don't own a lot of furniture. Only books and a few odds and ends were damaged. I guess I was lucky."

"That must have been a relief." With a sidelong glance at the staircase, she sighed and asked, "What did you have in mind for tonight?"

Brady contemplated the contrast between the food he had planned for dinner and the tasty, calorie-filled hamburger and fries they'd eaten the other night at McDonald's. Suddenly unsure of his dining choice, he hesitated. "I thought you might enjoy a vegetarian dinner. There's a new Indian restaurant that opened recently in Woodland Hills."

"Sounds good to me. As long as I don't have to cook, I'll eat almost anything." With a rueful smile, she laid her purse on an end table. "I confess Max has gotten to me, in spite of my good intentions to be firm. Let me go say good-night to him—I don't want him to think he's in trouble for asking to come along. I'll be with you in a minute.''

Max was lucky to have a mother like Jenny, Brady reaffirmed as he watched her disappear up the stairs. Would the kid feel lucky having him for a dad?

"NOT MUCH LIKE McDonald's, is it?" With interest, Jenny regarded the salad plate of sliced tomatoes, green peppers, cucumbers and eggplant caviar drizzled with vinegar and oil. A platter of hot bread flecked with garlic and cheese accompanied it. Still to come were the dishes suggested by the friendly waiter—spinach fritters, curried okra and fried Indian sweets for dessert. Her taste buds watered as she picked up her fork.

"I hope you like this type of food." Brady took a sip of the wine offered by the wine steward and nodded his approval.

"Like it? I love it!" She dug right in and chewed happily. "Hamburgers are great, but this is a welcome taste experience for a change."

Brady was relieved when he saw the enjoyment reflected on Jenny's face and her dimples dance in her cheeks. Since he'd made up his mind to see her and Max often, it was a welcome sign that he wasn't going to be expected to spend the rest of his days eating fat-laden hamburgers.

"Now, what is it you wanted to speak with me about?" Jenny emptied her coffee cup with a sigh of contentment and shook her head when the waiter inquired if she wanted a refill. "It's certainly a lot quieter here than at McDonald's or at the day-care center, isn't it?" She smiled playfully across the table at him. "I really appreciate a date with a grown-up." She gestured at the dimly lit room, where soft music played and guests spoke in hushed tones. "Especially in a place like this."

"Maybe we can do this more often," Brady replied, gazing over the rim of his wineglass at Jenny. Her lips curved in a satisfied smile that reached her eyes. Instinctively he smiled back, surprised at the glow of pleasure that spread over her face. The more he saw of her, the more he realized she was the most womanly woman he'd known since his Aunt Ellie had passed away.

Where had that thought come from? he mused. This was supposed to be an evening of scientific discussion, not a seduction. Although for some reason, scientific theories that used to absorb him seemed to have taken a back seat to his preoccupation with Max.

When their gazes locked, he wondered who was seducing whom, before he managed to push the thought away. It had been a long time since he'd reacted to a woman this way, if ever.

"I can't imagine how I can be of any help to you in your research," Jenny said as she moved her empty coffee cup out of the way and studied the patterns she was making with her spoon on the linen tablecloth. "But as long as you think so, go ahead."

"It's really just an exchange of ideas," Brady explained, grateful for the change of subject. Maybe it would cool down his errant thoughts. He took a small notebook out of his shirt pocket and cleared his throat. Not that he wanted to impress her in the way little boys tried to impress little girls. Jenny was definitely not a little girl, he reaffirmed as he took in her shapely form. He had to force his mind back to the subject at hand. "You may not agree with me, but my research has shown that a person has a better chance of succeeding and having a productive life if he has superior inherited abilities."

He was taken aback when he saw her blink and focus on him. On second thought, maybe he had sounded a bit pompous.

"You're talking about having the 'right stuff.'" Jenny's smile disappeared as she frowned and shook her head. "And that education and environment have little to do with a child's success in life. I've heard all that before. You're absolutely right—I don't agree." The look in her eyes dared him to argue with her.

"What do you mean, you don't agree?" Brady frowned, too. "There have been countless empirical studies that have proved I'm right!"

"And I'm sure there are just as many that prove you're wrong. Sorry," she said and dismissed his statement, "as far as I'm concerned, it takes a great deal more than the right genes to make a happy, well-rounded child."

"I gathered as much from the television interview you gave after the quake," Brady said, "but statistics show—"

"Children are more than mere statistics," Jenny stated firmly, becoming more and more annoyed. In order to get her advanced degree in elementary education, she'd listened to, and had had to accept, a lot of such foolishness in college, but she didn't have to accept it from Brady. "As far as I'm concerned, there can't be enough nurturing to help a child succeed. I see it happening every day at my school."

"Come on, how about the findings in *The Bell Curve?*" Brady insisted. "The authors are highly respected scientists. The study proves that high IQ scores are due more to genetics than environment and are almost impossible to change."

"A study that may prove something to you, but not to me," Jenny said shortly. "IQs aren't the only measure of potential."

"Then what about Max? He was smart as a whip. I'll bet his IQ goes off the charts. Can you truthfully tell me that's not important?"

Jenny's pleasure in her dinner started to evaporate. Max? How did they get on that subject? She looked Brady right in the eye for a long, silent moment. How could he be so dead serious about the theory after it had caused so much controversy? If it was because he was a genius himself, he was a close-minded one. And he needed a big dose of reality.

"From what you've told me," she said, leaning forward to meet his eyes, "you obviously spend all your time in a laboratory trying to prove you're right, and associating with people who agree with you. How about spending some of your time looking at the issue from the other point of view?"

"But I am right," Brady said, trying—without much success—to take his eyes from the pink skin that peeked between the folds of her blouse.

Jenny followed his gaze, and flushed when she realized just how much of her was showing. She straightened sharply and gazed sourly at him. She wasn't out to win the argument by trading on her femininity.

"Just like a man," she said.

"Just like a woman," he rejoined.

They were at a stalemate.

"How about the findings of the institute?" Brady insisted, ignoring her comment. "All the sperm in its sperm bank comes from high-IQ donors. And all the children born of that sperm have turned out to have intelligence remarkably above average!"

"Sorry, children aren't racehorses. I don't believe in the selective breeding of genes. You never really know what you're going to get. Not all geniuses grow up to be fine people," she said with a scowl. "What's the matter with having a normal, happy child?"

"Not a thing, if that's what you want. But these are alternatives available for a woman whose husband can't provide fertile sperm. Or if she doesn't have a husband. As far as health is concerned, at our institute the potential sperm donor has to provide a ton of information about himself. Hell, the questionnaire he has to fill out is twelve pages long!''

''More isn't necessarily better,'' Jenny parried as she studied Brady. He looked flushed and oddly defensive. A light dawned. Had he contributed to the sperm bank? Is that why he knew so much and felt so strongly about it? If he had, it was going to be his secret. It was about the last thing she cared to ask a man.

''I'm sure the success with those children is largely due to their parents' loving care!'' she went on. ''Who else but highly motivated, conscientious people would apply to a sperm bank such as your institute's?''

''Come on, Jenny, you're just being stubborn. What would it take for me to prove it to you?''

''Not a thing,'' she shot back. ''As far as I can see, you have a preconceived notion of what children ought to be and what they should be able to do. A normal, healthy child is what most people, including myself, want. As for you, if you'd get yourself out of the lab once in a while and spend some time around children the way I have, you'd see I'm right.''

''Okay, I will,'' he vowed. ''That's a deal. Starting tomorrow. And when I come over to the day-care center, I'm going to bring some studies for you to look at.''

With the issue of Max temporarily put aside, his scientist's antenna was quivering at the challenge. He had dozens of studies that would prove he was right. If only she wasn't so pigheaded! At that very thought, his earlier ardor cooled.

"Be my guest," Jenny said with a flourish. "You can talk your head off while you fix the hinges on the door. And maybe do a few other little odd jobs if you're up to it. But let me warn you, you're bound to be disappointed if you believe you can convert me to your way of thinking. I've been a teacher of young children too long. I know better."

Brady put his notebook back in his pocket as they traded irritated glances. It was just camouflage anyway. He'd remember everything Jenny told him—and a lot more. He'd remember the way her almond-shaped blue eyes flashed with fire when she was angry, the determined expression on her face and the set lips that told him she was definitely annoyed.

Jenny believed in nurture as strongly as he did in nature. Unless he was mistaken, it appeared they might never agree on the subject that was so important to him.

He opened his mouth for one more parting shot, when suddenly she started coughing.

"What's wrong?" he asked in alarm.

"Nothing," she managed to sputter between bouts of laughter. "It just occurred to me how ridiculous this conversation is. Whose children are we arguing about anyhow?"

He shut his mouth. He couldn't answer the question, not when he realized they were getting onto personal grounds. He wasn't about to give himself away.

"Tell me more about your school, Jenny," he said, deciding to change the subject before things got completely out of hand. After all, the last thing in the world he wanted to do was antagonize her. There was Max to consider, and besides, she looked damn sexy when she was riled up. She was a dangerous opponent. "How long have you owned it?"

"Long enough to know that children blossom if you're honest with them and show how much you care for them."

"Even without getting paid for it?"

"*Especially* when I'm not getting paid for it." She looked him squarely in the eye, daring him to argue with her. "Those are the children who need me the most. As far as charging, there are enough paying students to make up for the rest. No child brought to me is going to do without day care if I can help it."

Brady held up his hands in a gesture of surrender. It seemed they weren't going to agree on anything tonight. Not that it really mattered. There would be other times to discuss his scientific theories—maybe tomorrow when he'd try to fix the door to the nursery school.

"Let's declare a truce for now," he said with a wry smile. He held out his right hand, although under the tablecloth he'd superstitiously crossed two fingers of his left hand.

"WHERE'S MR. MORGAN, Mommy? You said he'd be here bright and early!"

"Now, Max. That's the fourth time you've asked me that question. 'Bright and early' could be anytime this morning." From where she was duplicating animal outlines for the children to color on Monday, Jenny cast an amused glance at her son. He couldn't seem to contain himself while waiting for Brady to show up. It was obvious some kind of chemistry had developed between them. "Here, you can start to color in this page."

"But when *is* he coming?" Max persisted.

"Soon, I'm sure."

"But when?"

"Now, Max, Mr. Morgan appears to be a very reliable person."

"You mean he's dependable?"

"Yes." Jenny gazed fondly at the impatient boy. Sometimes he sounded more adult than a lot of adults she knew. "If he said he'll be here, I'm sure he'll be here soon." She glanced at her watch. "It's only eight-thirty. I'm willing to bet the man is never late."

"Late for what?" a deep male voice asked from the door to Jenny's office.

In tight-fitting blue jeans that hugged his narrow waist and long legs, and a pullover sweater the color of his golden brown hair, Brady looked twice as handsome and three times as cool as he had last night. This time his tennis shoes fit right in with the rest of his outfit. In one hand he held a small, red toolbox, in the other, a bulging briefcase. Jenny stared while Max threw himself at the newcomer.

"You came, Mr. Morgan. You came!"

"Of course." Brady looked down at his mirror image. "I promised, didn't I?"

"Yeah. Mommy said you were reliable and she was right!"

"She said that, did she?" *Well, at least she thought there was something good about him.* "Ready for action?"

Delighted, Max eyed the toolbox. "Can I really help?"

"Sure," Brady answered. "Just let me come in and we'll set up our line of attack on the door." With Max clinging to his leg, he made his way into Jenny's office. "Good morning, Jenny."

"Good morning to you, too," she answered lightly. The way he'd said it sent erotic thoughts racing through her system that made her wonder if a "good morning" greeting had been all they'd exchanged. His low, baritone voice, coupled with his very striking male persona, gave her pause. This was all wrong, she told herself. His appearance here at the day-care center was strictly business and on a volunteer basis. Nothing personal.

He was here to fix the front door, and maybe a few other things. That is, if the toolbox was more than a prop. And, of course, to try to persuade her to see it his way about genetic influences. As far as she was concerned he was dead wrong. He wasn't going to be able to convert her to his way of thinking. If the man thought trading on his masculinity was going to soften her up, he had another thing coming.

She watched through doubting eyes as he put the toolbox on her desk, opened it and gently extracted Alfred. The bear's right ear was held together with a Band-Aid. She tried to suppress a giggle and failed.

"I don't know what's so funny." Brady looked offended at her reaction. "Alfred needed help and that's all I could think of. Besides, you did say you could sew and would sew up his ear."

"And you said you knew something about carpentry," she managed as she took Alfred and patted him on his little stuffed rear. "Do you have anything in there resembling tools, or was the toolbox just to transport Alfred?"

"Of course I have tools. I only carried the bear in there for safekeeping." He dug into the toolbox and held up a hammer, a small knife and a screwdriver. A plastic bag held some nails.

"You're going to try to fix the door with those?" Jenny was almost beside herself with laughter. It didn't take a genius to know he'd hidden Alfred because he was too embarrassed to be seen carrying a teddy bear. She could understand that. But these were tools? Were all scientists as impractical as Brady?

"I'm going to try."

He appeared offended, but she couldn't stop laughing.

"I do have a few things in the car in case I need them," he added as she caught her breath.

"What exactly do you do with that knife anyway?" she asked as she wiped a tear from her cheek. "It doesn't look as if it's going to be of much use."

"Oh, that. It's a carving knife. My uncle taught me to carve small wooden figures out of balsa wood with it. I brought it along just in case."

"The last thing I need is a 'just-in-case problem,'" Jenny muttered gazing at the toolbox. "I hope you have something more practical in there."

"Don't worry. Max and I are going to reconnoiter the area. If I don't have what it takes, I'll go to the hardware store and get it."

He had what it took, all right. Whether it was as a carpenter—that was another story. Jenny smothered a giggle as Brady led Max out of the office by the hand.

She gazed after Brady and Max for a long moment before she turned to the task of mending Alfred.

"Well, Matilda, what *do* you think of Brady Morgan?" Jenny straightened the ribbon in Matilda's hair before she went back to carefully peeling the Band-Aid from Alfred's ear. Seated on a small chair in the midst of teddy-bear country, Jenny searched for answers to her reactions to Brady Morgan. "I thought it might be easier on Alfred if I operated on him in the midst of friends to keep him company. Right, Alfred?"

With no answers forthcoming to her questions, Jenny finished the "operation" and sat back to survey her bear menagerie. Matilda's frown was serious; she hadn't taken the question about Brady lightly. The Cisco Kid in particular appeared troubled. Well, maybe they were right. She knew little if anything about Brady, except that he was a mad scientist and he appeared taken with Max.

She'd handle one day at a time and keep her mind and her ears open. After all, she reasoned, good looks weren't everything, and while the man had more than his share, he also had a few strange habits that would bear watching.

HOLDING HIS SCREWDRIVER, Brady carefully went about inspecting the front door. The top would have to be set back into the frame, but even from his limited experience it seemed to be a simple matter. All that was needed was common sense and a big dose of good luck. At his feet, Max happily hammered away with a toy rubber hammer.

"Careful, fella," Brady said when the boy became too enthusiastic and caught Brady in the ankle. "I won't be able to finish the job if you break my leg."

"Aw, Mr. Morgan, I wouldn't do that!"

"Tell you what, why don't you pick up the loose screws and hold them for me while I take care of the door?"

"That's not a real job," Max protested. "I want to help fix the door!"

Brady glanced over to where Jenny was mingling with her animal friends. If Max somehow got hurt, she'd have his head. "It's a very important job. How can I fix the door if the screws are missing?"

Max considered the idea. "Okay, but first I have to go to the bathroom." He scampered away.

Brady went back to work.

"Need some help now that your assistant is taking care of more important business?"

Brady looked at the arm that reached under his shoulder to catch a screw before it fell. Long, tapered fingers, their nails lightly manicured with rose polish, brushed the back of his hand in passing. He blinked. No way could he ask her to help. If he did, he wouldn't be able to keep his mind on business. And if she kept touching him, he couldn't answer to the consequences. He backed away. "Not really. I think I'd better wait for Max. I wouldn't want him to feel his help isn't valuable."

Jenny nodded gratefully. "Thanks for including Max. He's a wonderful boy."

"He certainly is." *And so is his mother.*

"I'm back, Mr. Morgan!"

"And just in time," Brady answered with a grateful sigh.

"Did Mommy help you, too?"

"She offered, but I saved the real work for you," Brady said, glancing over his shoulder to where Jenny had gone back into her office. Over in the corner, Alfred was having a family reunion. "You're a lucky kid to have a mother like her."

"Where's your mother, Mr. Morgan?"

"Somewhere in Egypt, the last I heard. I don't see much of her. She and my father travel a lot."

"Gee, that's too bad." Max frowned for a moment before his face brightened. "I have two mothers. Maybe you ought to get another one, too."

Chapter Five

"Two mothers?" Hand poised in midair, Brady turned to look down at his small helper. He took another quick peek into Jenny's office to make sure she wasn't listening, before he turned back to the boy. "Where's the other one?"

"She's in heaven. Mommy told me not to feel bad, 'cause I have her to take care of me. She loves me a lot. I know, 'cause she tells me so all the time."

As he gazed down at Max's trusting face, Brady felt moisture start at the back of his eyes. The child displayed an amazing maturity for a four-year-old. Maybe he *was* too young to fully understand the premature loss of his birth mother, but he certainly was a well-adjusted kid. And maybe in his case, Jenny was right about nurture being so important.

Brady's sixth sense tingled. Without realizing it, Max had handed him an answer to another one of his unspoken questions—why there was no discernible resemblance between Max and Jenny. Max had been adopted.

There remained only the crucial question of who Max's father had been.

Judging by the love he'd seen shining from Jenny's eyes whenever she spoke of or looked at Max, she might not have been the boy's biological mother, but she was his mother just the same. Once again he thought what a lucky kid Max was.

Brady had only to look at his own childhood to see why. He had a biological mother, sure, but that's where motherhood had ended. She'd arranged for his needs, but she'd never given much more than a fleeting thought about him. Dead civilizations and long-lost tribes fascinated her more.

"Do you remember anything about your father?" Brady hated to pump the kid, but the answer was an important piece of the puzzle.

"No." Max picked up a door screw from where it had fallen on the floor. "Gee, Mr. Morgan, this one is crooked."

Brady solemnly studied the damaged screw in Max's hand. "You're right," he announced. "That's probably why the door didn't hang right."

"Got any more screws with funny heads in your toolbox, Mr. Morgan?"

"Maybe. Why don't you take a look?" Brady answered when he saw the wistful expression on the boy's face. The kid was obviously dying to get into his toolbox, but was too polite to ask. Brady waited for a moment before he repeated what he'd asked earlier. He had to get the kid back on the question whose answer meant so much to him. "You're sure you don't remember anything about your father?"

"Mommy says he went to heaven before I was born. But she said he would have loved me, too."

The delighted expression on Max's face as he regarded the toolbox told Brady he'd done the right thing in asking Max to search for the correct screws himself.

"You bet he would have," Brady replied. How could the man have helped it? Who wouldn't fall in love with a child whose innocence showed in his eyes and came through in his voice? Brady had to restrain himself from picking up the boy and giving him a hug.

"Do you have a little boy of your own?" Max questioned as he happily rummaged through the toolbox.

Not yet, Brady thought as he reached for the small carving knife before Max could pick it up and cut himself. "No, but I sure wish I did."

"Well, I s'pose we can pretend I'm your little boy sometimes."

"Maybe we'd better not," Brady cautioned hastily. He could picture Jenny's reaction to that. Even if he survived her scathing remarks, his search for fatherhood would be over before it had barely taken off.

"I guess you're right, Mr. Morgan. Mommy doesn't like me to get too friendly with strangers anyway." He looked up at Brady and a thoughtful expression came over his face. "You're not a stranger anymore, though, are you, Mr. Morgan?"

"Not if I can help it," Brady responded, observing a small hand inching its way back to the toolbox. "Better watch what you're doing. There are dangerous tools in there.''

"I'll be careful—I promise. I just wanted to see what's inside.'' Max sat back on his heels and gazed up at Brady. "I wish I had a toolbox of my own like yours,'' he said wistfully. "And real tools. Mine are made of rubber.''

Brady added a red toolbox, a miniature screwdriver and hammer to the list of items he planned on buying for Max. "As a matter of fact, I hope we're going to be good friends.''

"Mommy, too?''

"Yes, Mommy, too.'' While he felt enriched by the pleased smile that came over Max's face, he was surprised to find himself imagining plans that included more than friendship with both Jenny and Max. The idea shocked him. He really didn't want Jenny in his life, did he? Up until now he'd been a workaholic with nary a thought of making any serious commitments that would take him away from his comfortable life and interesting research. How could he be thinking of taking on fatherhood and all that went with it? Even, to his amazement, planning to pursue Jenny, if only to satisfy an unnamed hunger?

Jenny was a complex person whose ideas differed from his own. He already knew how she felt about him, and it wasn't all that complimentary. She had no patience with his methodical personality and had made it clear she thought he lived in an unreal world with blinders on his eyes.

He'd discovered that where he was pragmatic and deliberate in his ways, she was spontaneous and given to purely subjective thinking. Like oil and water, they'd never mix. They were so different they could have come from different planets. If they ever connected they'd probably spend their time arguing.

Maybe he should have his head examined just for thinking seriously about taking up with her.

He turned his attention back to Max. He'd have to take one day and one cautious step at a time with Jenny or he'd be in trouble. That was more in keeping with how he operated anyway. He'd never made a snap decision in his life until now. And anything else made him feel uncomfortable. "So, did you find any screws with a cross in their heads in there?"

"Some." Max held up half a dozen for Brady's inspection. "Is that enough?"

"More than enough. You can hold the door for me while I screw them in. Let's put the small ones back." Max looked doubtful but reluctantly replaced the extra screws. "That's a good fella. Now take hold of the door."

"Stop right there!" an anxious voice called from across the room. Jenny rushed from her office. "Max, just what do you think you're doing?"

"I'm helping, Mommy," Max said, peering from around the door.

"Max, come here this minute! *I'll* help Mr. Morgan," Jenny added. "You go into my office this minute and put one of each of the papers on my desk in everyone's cubby for Monday morning's drawing lesson.''

"Drawing lessons?" Brady asked. "Aren't the kids a little young for that?"

"We only try to teach them self-expression," she answered, giving Max a firm look, "but right now we're talking about something more important—age-appropriate jobs. Holding up a door isn't something Max should be doing."

"Aw, Mommy, I want to help. I'm a big boy now. Besides, Mr. Morgan said it was all right."

"And I'm saying it's not! Into my office—right now!"

When Max stubbornly balked, Brady said in a stern voice, "You'd better do what your mom tells you."

Jenny waited while Max made a face, then with a shrug of his little shoulders slowly made for the office. When he cast one last, appealing look over his shoulder, she shook her head. Feet dragging, he disappeared.

She was becoming annoyed. This was the second time Max had obeyed only after Brady had told him to. Max was *her* son and Brady was a stranger. Who did the guy think he was? The more she thought about it, the angrier she became.

"Max is only four years old! He's still a baby!"

"He's a growing boy, Jenny," Brady insisted. "He needs to learn male things. Carpentry is one of them." He watched mixed emotions cross Jenny's face. Maybe reminding her her son was growing up wasn't the most diplomatic thing to do, but Max had to learn how to be a boy before he could become a man. Just as Brady had learned with the help of a loving aunt and uncle.

"I don't care about your opinions. As far as I'm concerned, he needs to learn responsibility first."

She seemed so upset Brady expected to be thrown out on his ear. He opened his mouth to defend his position; it was too late. She was on a roll—he couldn't get a word in edgewise.

"You ought to know better than to let him hold up a door that's ten times his size!" she continued as she turned her full wrath on Brady. "It could have fallen on top of him!"

"Not really. He only thought he was helping me. I knew the door was still partially attached to the doorjamb." He gave her his best apologetic smile, but she didn't appear to buy it. "But you're right. It's better to be safe than sorry." Brady felt like a jerk. "I guess I have a lot to learn about children, don't I?"

"You bet, and you'd better start learning right now. Especially if you're going to be around my son." Jenny glared at Brady from where she was holding on to the door. "Max might have been willing to help, but it takes a grown man—or, in this case, a grown woman—to do a job like this."

"Hey, I said I was sorry." Brady scowled back. "Let's declare a truce and get the door hung. We can argue later about whether or not I'm a grown man."

"I never said you weren't a..." Jenny felt herself color as she realized the interpretation he'd put on her flip remark. She took in all six feet of her volunteer carpenter. Tall and slender, dressed in working jeans and a sweater that did wonders for his broad shoulders and long arms, he was the ultimate male. "Sorry," she said under her breath. "I didn't mean to come on so strong. But where Max is concerned ... I guess I got carried away."

"Mothers are like that, I suppose," Brady said off-handedly.

"You suppose? Don't you know?" Jenny regarded him quizzically. "You *do* have a mother, right?"

"Sure, somewhere out there." He paused. "Max told me he has two mothers. You and ... ?"

"Some other time," she answered shortly. "Let's get on with the door."

She met his amused gaze. No matter how annoyed she was with him, she sensed there was something between them, something that didn't happen very often between people. Something she hadn't intended and didn't intend to happen now.

There had never been any doubt in her mind that Brady was a grown man—and one she was greatly attracted to at that. But the last thing she wanted at the moment was for him to know it. She turned her head before she gave herself away.

Brady was secretly pleased with himself. He knew by now that her bark was worse than her bite, and that he'd gotten to her, even if he hadn't planned it that way. He could tell by the blush that came over her face as she tried to avoid his eyes that her mind was on the same track as his.

"No harm, no foul," he said. "Max is perfectly okay, although I can't say the same for this door. Do we get it rehung or don't we?"

Jenny put her weight against the door as he set a fresh screw in the latch still attached to the doorjamb and went to work. She tried her best to ignore him, but it wasn't easy when he was only inches from her. In fact, it was darned near impossible, especially when she was so aware of his masculinity.

The angle of his lithe body as he reached up with both hands to work on the latch drew her fascinated gaze. Her eyes widened when his jeans hovered at his narrow waist for a moment before they slipped an inch and the waistband of his boxer shorts made its appearance. She held her breath when he forcibly turned the Phillips-head screwdriver and his body movements caused his jeans to slip again, this time revealing an inch or two of pale flesh.

Jenny tried to put the tantalizing sight of his bare skin out of her mind and to concentrate on something less disturbing. Hopefully, the repair would be over soon and he would leave, taking temptation with him.

She reconsidered when he raised his hands higher and more flesh was exposed. Maybe there were a few other odd jobs that she could have him take care of.

"There!" Brady exclaimed as he executed a final twist of the screwdriver and stood back to inspect his work. The door hung straight. "You can let go now."

"What?" Jenny had to force herself to try to forget the glimpse of his bare flesh and focus on his voice. Thank goodness his jeans and sweater were back where they belonged. Still, her gaze kept wandering to the black leather belt that should have kept his jeans in place.

"I said you can let go now."

"Are you sure? I wouldn't want the door to come off and fall on someone."

"It won't!" Brady managed not to look offended at her question. "If there's one subject I know well besides genetics it's carpentry. I have an uncle who insisted I needed a hobby, and he was right on the money. It's a great way to get rid of excess energy."

Get rid of excess energy! The pictures that came to her mind were like those of forbidden fruit: strong, sensual and with a hint of danger.

Jenny took a deep breath and stepped back; the door held firm. "Great. Hang on a minute while I go to the office and get a key."

Brady neatly arranged his tools in the toolbox until she returned with a chattering Max in tow. He watched with interest as she twice opened and closed the door before she tried locking it. Her caution puzzled him. After all, she should have known by now that he wasn't the kind of guy to do a half-baked job. His motto was Anything Worth Doing Is Worth Doing Well.

"You were right," Jenny commented, pretending to be satisfied the door was operating properly, when her mind was elsewhere. "It does look as if you do know what you're doing."

"Did you have any doubts?" Brady questioned. He studied the room, trying to decide what new excuses he could come up with for hanging around the nursery school. He still need to work on solving the mystery of Max's missing father.

It was also beginning to seem as if he was as much taken by Jenny as he was by her son. His visits had become more than a case of finding out if he was Max's biological father. He couldn't get Jenny out of his mind. He wanted to know all about her: who she was; what her dreams, her hopes, her plans for the future were? And, before he took his head out to be examined, how he just might fit in with those plans.

"Any more odd jobs you'd like me to take care of?" he asked casually.

When she colored slightly, he wondered what he could possibly have said to make her blush.

"Well...there *is* the bookcase over in the back," Jenny said. How did he know she was planning to ask him to hang around? And what was behind his reason for asking? Was he able to read her thoughts? If so, *was* he aware of her physical reaction to the sight of his bare flesh? "When I checked this morning it was kind of rocky. Actually, it didn't look anchored to the wall."

"No problem," Brady said with a faint smile. Any reason to hang around the lovely Jenny was fine with him. "Why don't you show me?" Brady said, lifting his toolbox. Maybe things were going to work out to his satisfaction, after all.

Jenny led the way to the back of the room, where the teddy bears sat in a circle, silently enjoying their reunion with their recuperating friend, Alfred. Her pant leg brushed against Matilda in passing and knocked the bear to the floor. "Excuse me," Jenny said as she stopped to pick up the bear and soothed its furry little beribboned head. "I should have watched where I was going." How could she have, when she was so preoccupied by her volunteer carpenter?

She could have sworn there was an "I told you so" expression on Matilda's face. She took a second glance. Maybe her imagination was working overtime, but the knowing expression was definitely there. "Okay, okay," Jenny murmured. *It's not as if I intend to fall into the man's arms. I'm only taking advantage of his offer to get some small repairs done.* A sidelong look at the smirk on Alfred's brow confirmed he agreed with Matilda's opinion. "Traitors," she mumbled as she turned her back on her furry friends.

"Did you say something?" Brady glanced up from where he'd been inspecting the loose bookcase.

"I wasn't talking to... Oh, forget it." With a last cautionary look at the teddy bears, Jenny pulled herself together and joined him at the bookcase. Her hand brushed against his. A glance told her the skin tone of his arms was darker than that at his waistline. Was the flesh at his waist this warm? she wondered. And as soft?

And how would it feel when damp flesh slid against damp flesh?

Matilda and Alfred had been right. At the rate her thoughts were going, it wouldn't take much encouragement on Brady's part for her to be in his arms. Not when he kept looking at her as if he wanted something more from her than a brief hand-to-hand encounter.

"Talking to the bears again?"

"You could say that," Jenny answered nonchalantly as she rattled the bookcase to show him the loose corners. The harder she tried to ignore his physical presence, the more difficult it became.

In his own unaware way, Brady was all male. He had a lithe body, warm golden brown eyes and a smile that captured a woman's heart. She was more aware of him than if he'd been trying to deliberately capture her attention. He definitely had whatever it took to capture her interest. As easily as a spider catches a fly in its spiderweb, he'd caught her thoughts completely. As they exchanged glances, she hoped he couldn't read her mind this time.

"Getting any answers?"

"What do you think?" she shot back. The truth was, she'd been voicing her thoughts and mentally using the teddy bears as a sounding board. The bears were right. At the rate she was going, she was headed for Brady's arms as sure as an arrow sought its target.

Brady was different enough to fascinate her, as well as oddly appealing with his changing personality, appearance, even his faulty scientific theories. He was like no other man she'd known and she wanted more of him. Good Lord, she thought, catching herself before her fantasy could get too far. She had to stop thinking about the man. Especially since, outside of that light kiss of comfort during the aftershock, he hadn't done anything to show the attraction was mutual.

When she fell silent, Brady felt he had to try again. He put a sympathetic hand over hers. "I didn't intend to make fun of you, Jenny. I confess, since you gave me Alfred, he and I have had some interesting conversations, too. You were right. He's been great company. It helps to clear your thoughts, to talk to something, even a bear, when you don't have anyone around to talk to."

Was he making fun of her? She glanced sharply at him, only to meet a raised eyebrow and that appealing lopsided smile of his. He was teasing her, repeating the advice she'd offered when she'd given him Alfred as a companion. Yet he looked as pleased with himself as if he'd discovered a great truth on his own. Given time, maybe he *would* see the whole truth of human development.

"That look of yours doesn't mean we're about to have another argument, does it—or should we declare an official truce?"

Argument? Whatever had they disagreed about? Looking into his smile, she couldn't remember his saying anything important enough to argue about. She couldn't help but wonder at his question. "A truce," she heard herself answer. There *was* a certain appeal about him that kept her from staying angry with him.

Not that she really wanted to. He resembled Max so much when he wanted her approval. And as with Max, she was more than ready to give it. "Yes, let's make it a truce. I'd like that."

"Me, too."

When he gently squeezed her hand and that appealing smile curved at the corner of his lips, a warmth crept up her middle and to all points, east, west, north and south. Instinctively, without even a glance to make sure Max was occupied elsewhere, she raised her face to his, lips parted in an unconscious invitation. When it came, his kiss was sweet and gentle and lingered long after the truce was declared and accepted. A warm tide swept over her and threatened to carry her into uncharted waters. She closed her eyes, put her arms around him and leaned against his solid chest, strangely willing to follow wherever the kiss led.

When he took her in his arms and deepened the kiss, it felt as if she'd come home. She'd forgotten, if she'd ever actually known, how satisfying it was to have the warmth of a man's arms. He seemed to understand that she was a woman with a mind and wants and needs of her own. Before, in an earlier life, she'd been seen as just a marital partner—a possession. With no children to hold her there, she'd felt alone and unwanted. She'd finally made the decision to find a new life for herself.

She'd never allowed herself to depend on any man since. But in her secret heart she'd yearned for someone to watch over her. Not financially; she did well enough in that department. But someone who wasn't afraid to show he was capable of understanding her strength as well as the feminine side of her. Someone to love and cherish her.

Brady was the first man she'd allowed into her life since her divorce, and the first to show he wanted to understand her.

She began to smile inside. In the back of her mind, a soft voice whispered what a wonderful truce this promised to be. And how foolish it was to argue with a man she so clearly wanted and who wanted her, even if he hadn't said so.

"Gosh, I'm sorry, Jenny," Brady said when he finally broke the kiss, held her away from him and gazed into her eyes. "I didn't mean to do that. I don't know what came over me!" He wanted to explain that his action had been an impulse, to make sure she hadn't read more into the kiss than he'd intended. Except that he wasn't sure just *what* he had intended.

Rattled by the sudden change in Brady, Jenny shook her head. She managed a smile through the pain that came over her at his explanation and his troubled look. Maybe he was no different from most men after all. "Me, neither. But you don't have to apologize. I've heard even friends can seal a truce with a kiss."

"You're right," he said, giving her a hug. "Friends, it is." Suddenly he stared behind her.

"Are you and Mommy going to get married?" a small voice demanded.

"No," Jenny sputtered. She never knew what Max would come up with next; this last remark of his added to the flood of embarrassment that swept through her. "What gave you that idea?"

"You were kissing." Max earnestly regarded his mother and Brady. "Married people kiss a lot. I know—I saw it on television."

"Max! That's enough!" Since she only allowed her son to watch programs meant for small children, Jenny knew it had to be Cindy's viewing that was the culprit.

Out of the corner of her eye, Jenny could see Brady's raised eyebrows and incredulous expression. He seemed to be as taken aback as she was. Romantic notions assumed second place. She grabbed Max by the shoulders and prepared to have a heart-to-heart with him in the office.

"Well, if you're not going to get married, I guess it still means you and Mr. Morgan are friends," Max insisted, digging in his heels. "Maybe you can get married next week?"

"Max!" Jenny had to restrain herself from picking him up and carrying him out of the room. She shrugged helplessly as she put a restraining hand on the boy's shoulder.

Brady avoided Jenny's eyes while he struggled to regain his composure. The situation might have been comical if he hadn't still been moved by the kiss he and Jenny had exchanged.

If this was part of being around a boy as bright as Max, he'd have to watch his step. Fatherhood might be more complicated than he'd thought.

"So, maybe we can ask Mommy now, huh, Mr. Morgan?"

Max obviously wasn't ready to leave, thought Brady with a deep sigh.

"Ask me what," Jenny said as she tightened her grip on her son.

"Mr. Morgan needs to—"

"Have a friend," Brady hastily interrupted. What a mess he'd created for himself! No way was he going to let Max suggest just yet that he become a daddy, part-time or otherwise. Not when Jenny was such a desirable woman. He had to figure out just what he wanted from her, but first he had to reestablish their relationship on a more platonic plane before he could gain her confidence. First things first. Fatherhood could come a little later.

"Of course we can all be friends. There's always room for one more friend." Jenny exchanged a wry glance with Brady. The kiss between them had been special, something more than a mere declaration of friendship. Whether they'd wanted it to be or not. Sparks had arced between them, sending a myriad of wonderful sensations through her and igniting desire along the way. Desire lingered within her still.

Wicked instinct warned her she had best be careful or Matilda and her friends might turn out to be right. For her own sake, and for Max's, she would have to be watchful.

Chapter Six

Repairing a broken bookcase and a few loose chair backs was a piece of cake. Coping with their owner was another matter. Was he doing something dishonest? He didn't think so.

In the beginning, his sole intention may have been to learn more about Max's parentage. But that was before he'd been detoured by Jenny. She had a pair of blue eyes that put a spring morning sky to shame. Her gaze was honest and direct. She seemed to understand so much about him. It was as if she saw clear into his heart.

In truth, she was calling forth a part of him he'd forgotten, if he'd ever had it to begin with. He'd always scheduled his time and his days down to the hour. Filled his time with research and writing papers for scientific journals. But none of that seemed as important anymore.

Right now, all he could think of was an auburn-haired vision whose ideas and sensuality threatened his plans. And, in spite of her declared independence, one who obviously needed his help.

He sure hadn't expected to meet up with someone like Jenny.

From the looks of the schoolroom, sprucing it up was going to take more than one or two visits. He grinned. Repairs to the cracked steps, a loose sign and broken shelving would give him reasons to visit often. After he laid in a new supply of nails and sundry items, he intended to do just that.

Even so, he'd have to watch his step. It didn't take a genius to know Jenny Walker was a woman who played for keeps. At this stage of his life, no matter how much he was attracted to her, he wasn't out for something permanent. Besides, she deserved the best. She needed an old-fashioned kind of man, someone who would be with her all her life. He wasn't certain he was ready to be that man.

Trying to ignore his attraction to Jenny was difficult. Especially when he remembered how satisfying it had been to hold her in his arms. Her lips, when they'd parted under his, had been soft and warm. She'd tasted of honey, a sweet, cinnamon flavor that made him long to sink more deeply under her spell.

Did she wonder what he was up to? And if she found out, would she feel betrayed? He hoped not. He had to tread carefully, he thought as he pondered the dilemma. Jenny was his only chance of finding out more about Max.

He tried to collect his wayward musings. He had to think of Max, get to know him, find out about the boy's parents. Even though his feelings for Jenny were changing, he couldn't allow his attraction to her to detour him.

He rummaged in his toolbox for the proper-sized nails to secure the bookcase to the wall. Until now, with the exception of the little carving knife, he hadn't had much use for its contents: token nails and screws kept in neat plastic cases. He'd have to visit a hardware store soon if intended to do some real carpentry. His uncle had shown him how to carve animals out of balsa wood. There had been ferocious tigers, clumsy monkeys and delicate little fawns. His collection was quite large now, but he hadn't used the other tools for months.

When was the last time he'd carved something out of balsa wood to add to his collection? He couldn't remember. Lost in fond memories, he fingered the carving knife.

The schoolroom required more than toys. From what he could see, there were at least half a dozen little chairs that needed repair or replacement and tables that needed refinishing.

Sensing Jenny would be too proud to accept new furniture, he made a mental note to check prices on unfinished furniture. Refinishing chairs and tables and replenishing the school's supply of toys were things he looked forward to doing. They would be more of a game than a chore. Anything having to do with Jenny would be more than a chore.

He had accumulated weeks of vacation time. He'd apply for them right away. Maybe his uncle, retired now, could be persuaded to help at the school.

Brady paused, belatedly remembering the briefcase bulging with the scientific studies he'd brought along with him to prove his theories. He hadn't thought of them since he'd arrived this morning—not even once. And just when did he think he would be able to have a serious scientific discussion anyway, when he was already becoming more preoccupied with Jenny herself than with her ideas about nurture?

He couldn't believe the recent one hundred eighty-degree change in his life. Here he was, neglecting his research and spending time fixing up a nursery school and talking to teddy bears, of all things.

The few dozen books that sat on a small table behind him, waiting to be put back on shelves, were well thumbed, worn no doubt by countless numbers of storytelling hours. Children attending Jenny's school were fortunate. With the solid foundation she gave them, reading would become a habit. He knew from his own experience that a child who loved to read had a step up on the educational ladder.

He mentally added a catalog of children's books to his list of things to get for Jenny.

"Think you can take time out for lunch?"

"Lunch?" His attention distracted by the question, Brady looked over his shoulder at Jenny. Her almond-shaped blue eyes held a glimmer of laughter, and an amused smile hovered at her full lips. If ever a woman had the ability to get his attention, it was Jenny. He didn't know what about him amused her, but she could have asked him anything at that moment and he would have agreed. The hammer caught his thumb. "Ouch!"

"Here, let me see that."

Jenny reached for his hand and examined it. A few drops of blood gathered in the corner of his thumbnail.

"Hang on a minute." With murmured words of apology to the teddy bear, she reached over and took the blue calico bandanna off the Cisco Kid's neck. She wrapped it around Brady's thumb. "You'll live. Here, keep your hand up in the air. I'll be back in a minute."

"Back? Where are you going at a time like this?" She was treating him like a child and he intended to have a little payback time.

"Good grief," Jenny chided. "It's only a small cut. Take it easy. I'm going to get a wet towel to wash out your 'wound.'" She patted him on the shoulder as she passed. "Trust me. You're going to be just fine."

Brady winked at Cisco, Matilda and Alfred. Now that he had Jenny's attention, he intended to milk the situation for all its worth. Besides, he'd discovered how much he enjoyed being on the receiving end of Jenny's tender, loving care.

True to her word, Jenny was back with a small, cold, wet towel, which she wrapped around Brady's thumb. As she held his hand, he was aware of her gentleness. Too aware, his body signaled. He hoped he wasn't giving himself away.

"There. You'll be good as new in no time."

"Are you sure you know what you're doing?" Brady asked as he regarded his bandaged thumb with a frown. He didn't want the contrived emergency to end just yet. Besides, now that he'd discovered a legitimate way to make physical contact with her, he hated to have her let go of his hand. Not when the brush of her fingers against his was so satisfying. "Doesn't it need some kind of disinfectant?"

"Don't worry." Jenny rummaged in her pocket and drew out a package of Band-Aids. "I came prepared. Little accidents happen at least half a dozen times a day around here. Believe me, you're in good hands. I had to pass a first-aid course before I was granted a license to operate the school."

"What are you going to do with those?" Brady inquired in mock horror when he saw the miniature bandages covered with tiny teddy bears. Those were fine for little kids, not for a grown man. "You're not going to ask me to put one of those on my thumb, are you?"

Jenny suppressed a giggle at the wary look on his face. "Okay, if you don't think you can handle it, I'll do it for you." She took his hand back; the sparks started in again. "They'll make you feel better. The kids love them. They work every time, I promise. Come on, now," she said sternly, "hold your hand still. You're behaving worse than Max when he gets hurt. At least Max thinks Band-Aids are a badge of honor."

"Don't you have any of the grown-up kind?"

"No. You'll have to settle for these." Jenny held back her laughter with difficulty. Whether he intended it or not, no one she'd ever met could make her laugh as easily as Brady. His body language and the injured expression on his face could have been part of a comedy routine. Could he possibly be serious around his "injury"?

"No one says you have to wear it on your thumb for the rest of your life," she reassured him. "It's only until the bleeding stops and to keep the fingernail clean." She busied herself with applying the bandage, taking great care not to linger over the task. The less she touched him, the safer it would be for her. No way was she going to get involved with this man—not when he was still an unknown quantity.

Brady regarded the top of her shining auburn hair. The faint scent of roses lingered there. The soft, soothing sound of her voice teased his senses until they came alive. Her touch was feathery, but the pat on his hand that was intended to be reassuring shifted his thoughts to more erotic play.

What had started out as a game suddenly became something more. He wanted her as a man wants a woman. He turned his palm up to grasp her hand. Startled, she looked into his eyes. "Jenny, I..."

"Don't say it," she said, all of a sudden grown serious and quiet. "Not unless you mean it. And if you don't, better leave it unsaid."

Regretfully, he dropped his hand. She was right. He wasn't ready to be serious, to talk about deeper feelings. Time, he thought; he needed time.

"Now, how about some lunch?" she asked briskly as she gathered the wet towel and Cisco's bandanna. "I brought Max's favorite—peanut butter-and-jelly sandwiches. I have cold chocolate milk in the refrigerator to go with them."

"They're a favorite of mine, too," Brady commented as he watched Jenny tidy up. "But I had the distinct impression hamburgers were Max's favorite."

"Not really. Max may think he's fooling me, but I know it's actually the toy that comes with the Happy Meal that he's interested in. Everything else takes second place, and only after he checks out the new toy he gets each week."

"Every week? You mean he gets a new toy every Wednesday?" So much for thinking Max was toy deprived.

"He sure does. Max keeps posters of the latest toy series being offered and lists of the ones he wants to collect. As I said, it's the weekly toy that attracts him. He plans his collections very carefully. In fact, he's that way about everything he does. To the point of driving me crazy."

Organized like me. "Seems to me you have Max's number." Brady was grateful for the change in topic.

"Naturally—I'm his mother. Max is pretty bright, but he's still just a kid. If I couldn't stay ahead of him, it would be a sad story." She glanced over at the bears.

"Sorry, Cisco, I'll return your bandanna as soon as I wash and iron it. I'll have it for you on Monday."

Once again Brady was struck by the charming way Jenny treated the teddy bears. She had the imagination of a child, the brains of an adult and, apparently, the common sense to be both when the occasion called for it. It was a combination that fascinated him. She was like no other woman he'd ever met.

"Bring on the sandwiches." Brady joined her at one of the tables. He could see letters and numbers carved in the scarred oak surface. They reminded him of his uncle's coffee table. It seemed a shame to sand down the table surface, when it must hold so many memories. "In some respects," he said, running his finger along a trail of lopsided *ABC*s, "children are all alike, aren't they? My uncle has a coffee table with my writing on it."

"Yes, they are. And I wouldn't change them for anything," Jenny said fondly as she produced the peanut butter-and-jelly sandwiches. "Each new activity is an adventure for them, including learning to write."

"You mean you don't mind autographed tabletops?"

"Not at all. That's what small children do when they press too hard with their pencils. It's part of the learning process."

Brady regarded her over his glass of chocolate milk. He was learning a lot of things, too. Among them, that statistics on child development were based on children's behavior and achievements, sure, but that children were more than numbers on paper.

They were wiggly little bodies, curious eyes and smiling faces. He suddenly understood that Jenny could be right, at least partially. Seen through the eyes of a child, every day could become an adventure.

Was it possible Jenny was also right about the importance of nurture? Of course, that wouldn't make him all wrong—or would it?

"By the way, where's Max?" Brady glanced around the room, which was empty except for him, Jenny and the teddy-bear brigade. "Doesn't he want to eat lunch, too?"

"Playing outside on a tricycle. I'm afraid he hasn't the patience to sit still for very long. I told him he could take his sandwich with him."

"I was wondering if he'd like to come on a shopping expedition with me." At her sharp look of inquiry, he added hastily, "You, too, of course. That is, if you'd like to come along."

"Max isn't allowed to go anywhere without me," she answered. "I'm sorry, but the answer is no. Thank you anyway."

"There's a toy store not too far away from here," he ventured, hoping to coax her into agreeing. "I just wanted to pick up a few things for the school and I figured he's the resident expert."

"You're right about that—he is." She smiled as she looked down at the sandwich in her hands, fidgeting a moment before gazing at him across the table. "Perhaps another time. I don't feel right about letting you buy things for the school. There has to be another way."

"It seems to me an old-fashioned candy or cookie drive to raise money isn't going to do you much good," Brady persisted. "I've paid for enough cookies and candy bars I've never eaten to know what it takes to raise money. From what I gather, some of the kids' parents aren't in a financial position to raise money to help out anyway."

"That's true." Jenny sighed. "But I hate to have you make any donations. You're doing enough already."

"I'm having the time of my life," he protested, surprised to find out the statement was true. Outside of his research, he hadn't felt so excited about anything for years. Not since he was a kid, in fact. "Tell you what. In exchange for sharing your ideas on nature versus nurture with me, why not let me help you refurbish the school and buy a few other things?"

"'Refurbish' isn't the word." she sighed again. "I'm afraid we had very little to start with. But," she added as she straightened proudly, "we make up for the lack of toys with a lot of personal attention and games."

"Lucky kids." Who was he fooling? In spite of his earlier ideas about ability being based on genetic inheritance, he admired Jenny's determination to give the children a decent start in life. A caring nature like hers was something statistics hadn't taken into account.

At the troubled look in her eyes, he wanted to take her in his arms, feel the pulse in her neck race against his lips, have her lips open under his. Put a smile back on her face. And spend the next few hours keeping it there.

Common sense warned him not to say or do anything that might break the companionable mood between them. Not while he still wasn't sure whether he was ready to pursue any kind of a relationship with her. There were so many questions yet to be answered. Besides, he had a definite feeling that when she found out about his suspected relationship with Max, she'd believe he'd been using her to get at the boy. She would have been right at the beginning, but his quest has turned into something more. She was involved now, too. He cared enough about her never to knowingly hurt her, but he had to find out if he was Max's father.

"Well," he said finally when it seemed that she didn't feel comfortable about his taking Max on a shopping trip, with or without her, "I guess I'm almost through for the day. But if it's all right with you, I'll come back next Saturday and finish up."

"Wait a minute." An excited look passed over Jenny's face. "You can help me in another way, if you want to and if you have the time."

"Of course," Brady said, fascinated by the way her entire body had come alive. When her eyes sparkled as she tilted her head and gazed speculatively at him, his body responded to her unconscious sensuality. "I want to help. My job at the institute isn't exactly nine-to-five, so my time is my own."

"Okay, then. When the earthquake happened, we were studying the letter *C*. I always try to bring in someone whose occupation starts with the letter we're studying. How would you like to be the letter *C*?"

"How's that again?" Brady thought rapidly; no way was he the letter *C*. "I thought scientist starts with an *S*."

"I meant carpenter, you fool!" she said as her eyes teased him. "You could dress like a carpenter, show the kids your toolbox and tools and maybe make something simple for them!"

"Hey, that's not a bad idea," Brady said, thinking rapidly now that she'd set him on the right road. "I could even bring in a set of sawhorses and a saw!"

"Nothing electric, mind you," Jenny added, eyeing his bandaged thumb. "I wouldn't want you to get hurt any more than you already are."

"What, this?" Brady held up his hand and wiggled his thumb. "This is a whole lot of nothing."

"You don't say." Jenny's eyes accused him. "A few minutes ago you were acting as if you deserved the Purple Heart for being wounded in action."

"It's a wise man who knows when to quit," Brady assured her. He drained the last of his chocolate milk, wiped a few crumbs off his shirt and rose to his feet. "I'll be here. It will give me a chance to observe the kids, too. By the way, who were the letters *A* and *B?*"

"One of the children's fathers is an actor, a movie extra. He did a skit for us that involved the children."

"And the letter *B?*"

"We've been lucky on that one, too. Another father works in a bakery." She laughed as she recounted the episode. "He brought a small portable oven with him and he and the kids made miniature loaves of bread. It was a blast!''

Brady was impressed. "I don't know if I can top those performances, but I'm willing to give it a try." He stretched and made a show of cradling his injured left hand in his right hand. "It's not every day a man gets wounded in the line of duty. You don't happen to have a splint, do you?''

"A split! For a scraped cuticle?" Jenny shook her head in reproach. "Too bad we still aren't on the letter *A*. You make a darned good actor.''

"Well, if you don't think I need any further care, maybe I'd better move on. I have things to get ready if I'm going to come back for a carpentry demonstration. Let me know when you want the theatrics to begin.''

"Theatrics or a lesson in carpentry?''

"Carpentry." Brady gave an exaggerated sigh.

"Monday?''

"As soon as that? For a few minutes a while ago, I thought you might have wanted to see the last of me." He tilted his head and looked at her with a smile. "Friends?''

"We do have a truce, don't we?" she answered, caught by those golden brown eyes that reminded her so much of her son. "I haven't lowered the white flag yet. You're more than welcome.''

"In that case, I'll be here around ten o'clock. I have a few stops to make." Brady glanced through the window, where he could see Max pedaling his tricycle.

"Mind if I say goodbye to Max?" When Jenny nodded her approval, he saluted her with a brief smile, picked up Alfred and made for the school yard.

"Hi, fella! I came to say goodbye."

Max stopped pedaling. "You're not mad at Mommy and me, are you?"

"What makes you think so?" Brady crouched to meet the boy's eyes. He wanted to take him in his arms, hug him, never let him go. "It's just time for me to go home. I'll be back again on Monday with a big surprise."

"Promise?"

"I promise." Brady was beyond caring whether Jenny would object to a display of affection between Max and him. He reached over, took the boy's small face in his hands and kissed him on his forehead. "And you can bet I always keep my promises. Now, listen to your mother while I'm gone. Okay?"

"Okay."

The boy's mouth drooped as he managed a smile that captured Brady's heart all over again.

"But I wish you were staying."

"Me, too." Brady gave Max a fierce hug. "Here, take care of Alfred for me until I get back. See you on Monday."

"WELL, WELL. Two visits in as many weeks!" Ted Morgan shook his nephew's hand and motioned for him to come in. "Something important must be up."

Brady dropped into his favorite armchair and fondly regarded his uncle. Time had treated the man gently. He was still tall and stately in bearing, with graying hair that lay in soft waves across his forehead. His brown eyes were bright, and as usually was the case when they met, a smile curved his lips.

Brady berated himself for neglecting the man who was like a father to him. He'd thought of him constantly in the past two weeks, spoken of him admiringly, and had even found himself quoting him. Suddenly, with great clarity, Brady realized how much his uncle had taught him, had influenced his thinking, and how much he owed him.

"Would you believe me if I told you I missed you, Ted?"

Ted Morgan leaned back in his own armchair, rested his chin on his forefingers and laughed. "Suppose you tell me the real reason you decided to come over. Has it anything to do with that snapshot I carry in my wallet?"

"Not much gets past you, does it?"

"I'd be a sad case if it did."

Brady laughed. It was just about the same exchange he'd had with Jenny over Max. "I think I've heard those words before." He waved off his uncle's inquiring gaze. "I give up. You're right, as usual."

He went on to tell his uncle about the events that had transpired since he'd last visited. "The boy is mine, Ted. I feel it in my bones. Everything inside me tells me I'm his father."

Ted looked at Brady thoughtfully. "Maybe it's because you want it to be true. At any rate, I hope you realize that donating sperm doesn't make you more than a biological father. It takes more than that to be a real father. I hate to knock my own brother, but you ought to know the truth of that."

"Yes, I know. Once I find out Max actually is mine, I intend to *be* the same kind of father you are to me, Ted." Brady gazed affectionately at his uncle. Now that he'd fallen head over heels for a small boy with golden brown hair and eyes that matched his own, he could relate to the depth of feeling his uncle obviously felt for him.

Ted nodded. "I thank you for that, my boy. You're the son of my heart and I couldn't wish for a better one." The two exchanged smiles.

Ted cleared his throat. "Now, what about the boy's mother? What do you think she'll do when you ask her point-blank if her son's birth was the result of artificial insemination, and then tell her you believe you're the donor and the boy's biological father? And most important, how do you intend to go about proving it?"

"Actually, Jenny is not his biological mother." His uncle's raised eyebrows asked a silent question. "Max told me he was adopted, that both his birth mother and father are dead."

"That's not going to make it any easier for you to prove you're the biological father, you know."

"No, I'm afraid not. I'll have to persuade Jenny to tell me more about Max's parents. There has to be a clue in there somewhere. I won't give up until I know for sure he's not my son. But that's not the only reason I dropped in tonight.''

Brady went on to tell his uncle about his carpentry exploits. ''I was hoping you would like to help out around the school, too.''

''Just what did you have in mind?''

''I want to buy some unfinished small tables and chairs and paint them bright colors to match the school's and Jenny's personality.'' Brady stopped to smile at the thought. ''And build new bookcases and shelves to replace the cardboard boxes she calls cubbies that hold the kids' belongings.''

''Sounds like a good idea. Ambitious, but good.'' Ted laughed. ''Did you have anything else in mind?''

''I thought perhaps a tree house like the one you built for me.''

''Doesn't sound too safe, not with a dozen little kids wanting to use it at one time.'' Ted thought about it for a few minutes. ''How about something on the ground— a playhouse, for instance?''

''I don't know. How are we going to build a playhouse with all the kids milling around and getting into things? If any of them got hurt, Jenny would have my head!''

''Prefab, my boy. Almost everything comes ready-made today. We could have it up over one weekend when the children aren't there. The shelves, too.''

Brady grinned. A bright, new schoolroom with a playhouse to match sounded like a wonderful idea.

Both Max and Jenny were bound to love it. "I knew you'd have the answers, Ted. Jenny and Max will be delighted and so will the rest of the children.

He sat back and happily contemplated the idea. "I want you to meet Jenny and Max. Helping me ought to be a logical way to do that without arousing any suspicions. I'm sure once you lay eyes on the boy, you'll agree with me. He's the exact image of me in the snapshot in your wallet. It's positively eerie!"

There was a long moment of silence. Ted glanced over at the picture of his late wife before he smiled wistfully, looked back at Brady and nodded. "I'll be more than happy to help. I need a break from my latest book, anyway. You know, it would please me to give a couple of weeks of my time to be able to see you as a youngster again."

Chapter Seven

At precisely ten o'clock on Monday morning Jenny responded to a knock on the door. She had to take a second look before she recognized Brady in full regalia as a carpenter.

He wore a yellow hard hat and a wide leather belt that sported a variety of carpentry tools. In one hand he held his red toolbox. In the other hand was a small saw, its teeth covered by a leather guard. The saw was intended for show, she hoped. She'd never allow it near the children otherwise. At Brady's feet were half a dozen short planks of various shapes and sizes with nails partially inserted in each end. An older man stood beside him carrying a small, lightweight wooden sawhorse under each arm.

Brady looked ready, willing and, hopefully, able to be the letter *C*—or anything else she wanted of him. And, after some scrutiny, it was more than a carpentry demonstration that came to her mind. He looked great in his authentic outfit, but she was willing to bet he looked good without it, too.

Blushing at her wayward thoughts, she gazed at the man she'd considered a narrow-minded scientist until now. Jenny was caught up in the latest change in him.

The first time she'd laid eyes on the man, he'd appeared and behaved like a well-dressed, misplaced banker—even with those incongruous tennis shoes on his feet. Once she'd found he wasn't the earthquake insurance adjuster she'd been expecting, her first instinct had been to send him packing. Especially when he spouted theories and statistics about child development that were so different from what she believed in he'd set her teeth on edge.

All that was before she'd realized he was harmless and not half-bad-looking.

He certainly hadn't appeared half as attractive as he did today. Even when wearing an outfit that belonged at a construction site instead of in a schoolroom.

She wasn't sure what had caused the change in him, but whatever it was, he was different: softer, amusing and certainly more interesting. He might have said he wasn't ready for anything more than a few days of scientific observation, but from the way he kept eyeing her, she knew he was interested in a lot more. And judging from her physical reaction to the man, so was she.

The now-familiar warmth stirred in her middle. Goose bumps crept up her arms, her breasts and to the base of her neck. She hadn't been so aware of a man in years, and certainly never one who always looked romantic. Even now, yellow hard hat and all.

Brady gazed at the vision standing in the doorway to the Teddy Bear Center. She was dressed in her regulation blue jeans and white shirt, but today she'd covered it with a multicolored crocheted vest in green, blue, orange and gray. Her ever-present ponytail was caught by a matching ceramic clasp that, together with the vest, made her eyes bluer, her silken auburn hair more vivid, her skin more glowing. The wide smile that gradually lit up her face as they exchanged glances made his efforts to dress for the part he was to play worthwhile.

When her lips curved into that soft, welcoming smile, it was all he could do not to take her in his arms. He kept a tight rein on himself and stepped backward. But not before allowing his gaze to travel up and down her body.

She looked lovely, naturally soft and feminine and pleased to see him. He felt a little insecure, as if he were operating under false pretenses. His guilty conscience warned him he was no actor, and not much of a carpenter, either. Thank goodness his uncle was more or less the real thing.

As they exchanged glances, a not-too-surprising revelation swept over him. Jenny was a woman a man wanted to have in his arms and never let go.

In that one moment, he suspected it wouldn't have taken much encouragement for him to put aside his reservations about pursuing a relationship with Jenny.

With her hair caught back in that youthful ponytail and bobby socks and Reeboks on her feet, she once again looked like a schoolgirl not much older than her assistant Cindy, who was sitting on the rug in the background with the children, taking it all in.

"Hope we're on time," he said, feeling like a schoolboy himself. A schoolboy whose newly awakened hormones were working overtime. He wanted to tell her how lovely she appeared, how much he'd missed her. Instead he felt shy and tongue-tied.

"I never doubted you would be." Jenny took in the yellow hard hat and golden brown eyes that sparkled with good humor and excitement. And something else. She had to restrain herself from making a flip comment and breaking the sudden sexual tension that hung between them.

She glanced at the older man who stood at Brady's side. The resemblance between them was faint, but it was there all the same. Even to the shock of hair that fell over both men's foreheads.

She smothered her wayward thoughts and nodded her welcome. This was no time for erotic exchanges, and certainly not with an audience looking on and listening as avidly. "Good heavens, Brady, just what are you?"

"Your carpenter, reporting for duty," Brady replied.

"With a hard hat?"

"Safety First is a motto of mine. The kids might as well learn it's smart to wear a hard hat around construction sites."

"Construction sites?" Jenny covered her mouth before the laughter that bubbled up could spoil Brady's act. He couldn't possibly be serious. This all had to be a comedy routine. "Just what type of major construction were you planning?"

"Nothing big," he demurred. "It's just that I believe anything worth doing is worth doing well. Right, Ted?"

Jenny's gaze swiveled to the man at Brady's side. Laughter brimmed in his eyes as he solemnly nodded.

"Right."

"Jenny, this is my uncle, Ted Morgan. He's offered to be my backup man for a few days while we take on some repairs here. Ted, this is Jenny Walker."

"Don't you believe him, Miss Walker. He coerced me. I'd tip my hat, but..." He gestured with the sawhorses.

"We're glad to have you regardless, Mr. Morgan. And thank you for your help. Please call me 'Jenny.'" She stood back as he edged sideways through the door. "Can I help you with one of those?"

"Why don't you call me 'Ted.' And no, thanks. These are cumbersome but lighter than they look. I'll come back for the boards in a minute."

"The children have been waiting for you. They're so excited I could hardly keep them still. Not even the promise of an extra story hour could do the trick." She eyed the boards with the nails already in place at each end. "Why the nails?"

"Ted thought it would be a great experience for the kids if they took turns helping make a couple of simple foot stools," Brady explained. "He suggested we set the nails in partway so that no one will get any fingers hurt.

Now it'll just be a matter of letting the kids pound the nails in the rest of the way."

"Thanks, but I'm afraid we don't have real hammers," Jenny said regretfully. "Only the rubber mallets we use for wood jigsaw puzzles."

"No problem. We stopped to pick up a few small-sized hammers and some other items. If it's okay with you, the kids can take turns helping."

"I'm afraid you've come at recess time," Jenny apologized. "You'll have to wait while the children take turns going to the bathroom. We don't want accidents of any kind during the demonstration." She looked at Brady meaningfully.

"That's okay," he said as he winked. "We'll just set things up in the meantime."

Jenny led the way into the large schoolroom. As they passed the bulletin board, Brady paused long enough to draw his uncle's attention to the display of photographs on the wall. "Take a look at the kid in the top row center," he said softly.

Ted glanced at the pictures. "Good-looking kid. He does have your coloring and your smile. Still, he resembles a lot of other kids his age. I don't know, Brady. I think you should draw in your horns. We're dealing with real people here. I feel that someone is bound to get hurt." He shook his head. "Come on before Jenny misses us."

Round-eyed, bursting with excitement, the children hopped up and down on the communal rug like so many bunny rabbits let out of their cage. When they caught sight of Brady, they waved and giggled.

Max hurtled toward Brady and Ted. "Mr. Morgan, Mr. Morgan, you came back!"

Brady set down his toolbox and saw, and caught the small boy just as he jumped into his arms. It felt good to hug the warm, wiggling little body. A fierce protectiveness surged through Brady. He'd never known until now what he was missing, but he wasn't going to miss it much longer. "I promised I'd come back Monday, didn't I?"

"Yes, I know you did, but yesterday took forever!"

"Well, I'm here now." Brady moved Max's hair away from his eyes and smiled when it immediately fell back out of place. "Did you take good care of Alfred for me?"

"Yes, but he missed you, too."

Max peered over Brady's shoulder. "Did you bring your daddy to play with us?" he asked.

Daddy! Brady shared a smile with his uncle. "You might say that. His name is Morgan, just like mine. Ted, this is Max."

Ted set down the sawhorses and reached to grasp Max's warm little hand. "Hey, there, Max."

Over the boy's head, Brady caught his uncle's gaze.

Ted nodded slowly. "Max, my boy, somehow I feel I've known you for a long time."

Brady could see moisture gather in Ted's eyes.

A short time ago, Max had hesitated to shake hands with Brady. Now the boy not only welcomed him, he welcomed Ted, too. Touched by the measure of trust Max placed in him, Brady felt his own eyes filling with tears.

"Are you going to be a carpenter like Mr. Morgan?" Max eyed the sawhorses and the saw. "Wow, this is going to be fun!"

"I'm just here to help when he needs me. How about if I sit with you and watch?"

"I'll be right back. Wait for me!" Max dashed off to the bathroom. "Don't forget!"

"Well, what do you think of Max?" Brady asked quietly when Jenny followed her son.

"He's all boy," Ted agreed, "even down to that wicked little smile. Be careful. You wouldn't want to cause anyone any unnecessary pain, especially not the kid. Wait until you have proof before you try to claim the boy. Don't jump the gun."

"You're right, of course, but there's more to this whole thing than if I'm Max's father." Brady gazed over to where Jenny was helping the children wash their hands. "It's not only the boy, there's his mother, also."

"You're right. Something tells me she's not going to take this all in stride." Ted followed his nephew's gaze. "I don't think she wants ghosts coming back to haunt her."

"Probably not, but that's not what I meant." Brady felt himself flush. "It's more than that. I'm afraid she's gotten to me, too."

"Well, thank heaven for that." Ted laughed. "You know, you may be able to solve the whole problem more easily than you think."

"How's that?"

"Marriage. If you're that smitten with Jenny, why don't you consider asking her to marry you? She appears to be a fine woman."

"I've never thought of myself as marriage material, Ted." Brady glanced over at Jenny. He hoped she'd been too busy to overhear the conversation. She'd think he was up to no good. Maybe, in her eyes, he was.

"Take it from me, there's nothing like having a family of your own, especially if you can have a son like Max."

"I've been so involved with my work I haven't taken the time to think about marriage."

"Think about it." Ted looked over at Jenny. "From what you've told me and from what I've seen, it seems to me there's a warmth about the lady that no scientific research can match."

Before Brady had a chance to answer, Jenny came back to join them.

"We'll be ready in a few minutes."

"Hold up a minute. I brought you something." Brady opened his toolbox and handed Jenny a small, carved teddy bear. A wide smile curved its lips, miniature tiny pearls were set in its ears and a rope of pearls hung around its neck. On its round little stomach, he'd carved a heart.

"My, she's adorable! Did you make her?" When he nodded, Jenny examined the little brown bear that was hardly bigger than her hand. "When did you have the time?"

"Yesterday. She's just a little gift to thank you for letting me drop in."

Jenny was touched. "Little things mean a lot," she said, slowly running her fingers over the bear's face. She exchanged a warm glance with an obviously embarrassed Brady. From everything she'd seen, he was a good man with a tender heart. Somewhat misguided in his professional thinking, but good nonetheless. Good with children and, for that matter, with grown-ups, too.

She wished they were alone so she could let him further demonstrate how good he could be. She had a few ideas of her own, also.

"I'll have to consult with Matilda before I name her," she said as she tucked the tiny bear into her shirt pocket.

"Matilda?" Ted asked.

"She's a friend of Alfred's," Brady answered. When his uncle looked puzzled, he added dryly, "I'll explain later. Not that you'll find it easy to believe. You may decide I've lost my marbles, but all I ask is that you keep an open mind."

The children ran back by ones and twos and eagerly surrounded Brady. From the way they eyed the open toolbox and the hammers, he could tell it was time to begin.

"Okay, everyone," Jenny announced as the last child, Max, appeared. "Remember not to touch anything unless Mr. Morgan gives you permission. Take turns and no pushing or shoving, or you'll have to go back and sit with the Cisco Kid!''

When she turned back to Brady, she found him gazing at her admiringly.

"You remind me of my early boarding-school days," he said. "There were so many rules to learn I had a devil of a time trying to remember them."

"Children need rules. We all do," she answered before she returned her attention to the children. "Otherwise we wouldn't know what's expected of us. Now, children, remember what I told you. No one talks to Mr. Morgan while he's working or he might hurt himself."

She saw Brady glance at his thumb, look back at her and grin. The teddy bear Band-Aid was gone. The wicked grin on his face confirmed he had been playing on her sympathy before. Not that she'd minded; holding his hand *had* held a certain satisfaction.

"Now, children, Mr. Morgan will call you up three at a time," she said, changing the subject before Brady carried out the threat his grin promised. "Remember to do only what he tells you. Please sit down until Mr. Morgan is ready."

"That's a lot of rules for such little kids," Brady commented under his breath as he laid out the hammers.

"Those were only the beginning." Jenny pointed to a list of rules that hung on the wall beside them. "I have a few more posted up there."

"'Share your toys with your friends. Never hit other children or they might hit you back. Please and thank you are easy to say. Raise your hand before you talk,'" Brady read softly. There must have been at least twenty-five rules.

"These kids can read?"

"One or two, like Max. We go through the list every day. We let all the children each pick a favorite rule of their own and have them recite it when it comes up on the list."

"What's Max's favorite?"

"Number seven—'A place for everything and everything in its place.' And he's good at implementing it, too. Separating crayons by their colors and putting them in their proper containers is something he loves to do. Even at his age he's meticulous."

Brady and his uncle exchanged glances. She could have been describing Brady, as a child and now.

"Okay, let's have the first three children." Brady settled his leather belt around his hips. He felt more than ready, especially when his audience thankfully knew less than he did about carpentry. "Ted, how about distributing the hammers?"

With the children avidly paying attention, he fit the precut pieces together. One by one, the children took turns pounding in a nail, until several small crooked stools were finished. The happy expressions on the children's faces made him feel like a hero.

"All right, boys and girls," Jenny finally called when it looked as if the children had had enough excitement for the day. "It's time to wash your hands and get your lunches from your cubbies."

"We already washed our hands," a chorus of small voices protested.

"I know, but do it again." Jenny pointed to the large, rectangular porcelain fountain outside the bathroom door.

"What's next?" Brady inquired as the children scattered.

"Lunch, then nap time. But I don't think the children need any help with that." Jenny laughed as she kept an eye out for water fights. "You've exhausted them." She turned to Brady's uncle, who was packing up and getting ready to leave. "Thank you for coming with Brady, Ted. The children will remember today for a long time."

"And I will, too," Ted replied. "This was a lot more fun than teaching a class at the university. Your students are certainly a great deal more enthusiastic than the grown-up kind."

"That's what's so satisfying about being around small children," Jenny stated as she gestured to where small bodies pushed their way to cardboard cubicles and scattered to the tables with their lunches. "Everything is new and wonderful to them. I try to see things through their eyes, so it's been wonderful for me, too. You and Brady were great. They'll be talking about you for days."

"I'm glad. Say, Brady tells me there are a few things around here that need fixing. I'm kind of between projects and I've offered to help. Mind if I look around?''

"Not at all." Jenny hesitated before she added, "I don't know how to thank you enough."

"No thanks are necessary. As a matter of fact, today has been a two-way street. I feel richly rewarded by your allowing us to be here."

"Can I help you take things out to the van, Ted?"

Brady, hard hat gone and minus his leather tool belt, sauntered over. His brandy-colored hair was more awry then ever; his shirt was mussed. His tight blue jeans clung to his lithe body as if they'd been painted on him, and his slow, sensuous movements sent her senses whirling. She didn't know how she would be able to handle the rest of the morning in a sensible manner if he kept that up.

He was all male.

She found herself responding to a lazy smile that made her aware of suddenly taut breasts straining against her shirt and hormones that were on a rampage.

She'd known being around the children would loosen him up, humanize him, but she hadn't realized just how much. Nor had she known that her attraction to him would grow as his personality softened.

Just watching him fruitlessly push his hair away from his forehead sent a shiver of anticipation through her. He hadn't touched her, yet she could feel his hands stroking her all the same. Large, capable hands that would fuel the fire growing within her. Warm, tender hands that would take her to a place she couldn't remember ever having visited before.

Speechless, she worried her lip as she tore her attention away from Brady to his uncle.

"I have some sandwiches in the office refrigerator, Ted. Why don't you and Brady come into my office and share them with me? After the children go down for their naps, we can talk more about repairs."

"Sandwiches sound good." He gestured at the sawhorses. "Perhaps we should leave these here somewhere for more serious work?"

"There's a shed around back. The lock is broken, but you can leave your things in there, if you like. No one around here would take them."

"Great!" Ted replied, eyeing Jenny and his nephew. "I'll be back in a few minutes. Brady, why don't you and Jenny get together and decide what needs to be repaired next?"

Brady sensed his uncle was trying to give Jenny and him time together. Not that he minded, but judging from the clamor coming from the lunch tables, it sure wasn't the time or place for what Brady had in mind.

Jenny watched Ted leave before she turned her attention to Brady. This was no time for mental sensual wandering. Not when it wasn't going to lead anywhere. "You've done a wonderful job."

"Don't treat me like one of your kids," Brady said quietly, gazing into her eyes and dismissing the schoolmarm tone in her voice. "I'm a man, Jenny."

"Well, yes, of course." *How well she knew that!*

"And someday I'm going to show you what I mean," he said, glancing over at the children to make certain no one was watching before he took her hands in his. "In fact—" he paused as his gaze swept her flushed face "—I never knew how much I was missing until I met you. I'm looking forward to making up for lost time. I hope you feel the same way."

"The children!" she cautioned softly. "They can hear you."

"Well," he said, reluctant to let her off the hook just yet. "I can understand responsibility. But later. I promise." He ran his finger across her flushed cheek. "And I always keep a promise."

LATER THAT AFTERNOON, Jenny kissed Max goodbye when he left to spend the night with his best friend, little Tommy Cooper. An empty feeling swept through her as she contemplated a night without her son, but he was growing up. It was time to allow him the fun of overnights.

Before she could lock up the school, the doorbell rang.

"Hi." Minus his carpenter's costume, Brady stood on the front porch. "I'm glad you're still here. I forgot my carving knife."

Jenny gazed at him for a long moment. Forgetting anything was definitely not part of Brady's character. "I can't imagine how you could have forgotten something so important to you," she finally said, "but come in."

When Brady brushed by her, almost deliberately touching her as he passed, Jenny felt fairly certain he hadn't forgotten anything but rather that he'd remembered something. A promise. When he put his hands in his jeans pockets and grinned boyishly, she knew she was right.

"It looks as if everyone has gone home," he said, checking around the empty room with a slight frown. "Where's Max?"

"Staying overnight with a friend," Jenny answered. Why did her explanation sound like an invitation?

"In that case, how about dinner?" Brady asked, turning his inviting gaze on her. "Just the two of us again. This time, you can choose."

From the look on Brady's face, she was afraid it wasn't only dinner he was offering. When he tilted his head and used that lazy grin on her, she was sure of it.

"Maybe not."

"Did you ever do anything daring?" He took a step toward her. "Really daring?"

"Sure," Jenny replied warily.

"Like what?" He took another slow step.

Under his sultry gaze, and with his body only inches away, Jenny couldn't remember much about the morning, let alone events that might have taken place a lifetime ago. "I . . . I don't remember."

"Have you ever made love under the stars, for instance?"

"Stars?" she managed. She had the sinking feeling things were rapidly getting out of hand.

He nodded. "I didn't think so. If you had, you would have remembered."

Jenny pulled her thoughts together and backed away. "From the way you behaved when we first met, I would have thought you were too busy to think of something so frivolous."

"Frivolous?" he questioned. "That's a new one. I'm a research scientist, Jenny," he said as he followed her into the schoolroom. "I never said I was a monk."

Jenny gazed at skintight blue jeans, a muscular chest, broad shoulders and knowing eyes. "No, I guess you're not."

"So, how about it?"

"Dinner?"

"That's a good starting point," he answered with a smile. "We can take things as they come, or..."

"Never mind the 'or,'" Jenny replied in as firm a voice as she could muster. Thinking about sharing an amorous moment or two was one thing. Dwelling on making love under the stars was another. And putting either into action was a different matter entirely.

"It's dinner period. After all, we hardly know each other. I'll get my coat while you hunt up your knife."

"Knife? What knife? He looked confused at being reminded why he'd come back to the school in the first place.

"Forget it." Jenny laughed. "I never believed you'd forgotten it anyway."

"Then why did you let me in?"

"Why do you think?" she asked, gazing boldly into his eyes. It was no time to be coy, not when she'd spent the afternoon wondering if he really meant to keep any of his promises—and afraid that he wouldn't. As long as he realized she was onto him, she'd be okay.

"I think we'd better get started," Brady announced as soon as she had her coat on and her purse in hand. "The sooner we have dinner and get to know each other, the better. Any suggestions?"

"There's always McDonald's," she teased.

"No way! Only Max could drag me there!" Brady threw up his hands. "Try again."

"Well, there's a great deli not too far from here."

"Not private enough," he said, shaking his head. "I thought we could take this opportunity to really get to know each other."

"I suppose we could go to my place," she ventured. "I make a great Greek omelet. It would give us a chance to talk, if that's what you really want."

Really want? No way was he about to tell her what he *really* wanted.

"Then after you, ma'am. I'll follow you in my car."

He'd promised to show her later how he felt about her, Jenny thought as she gave the room a last minute, hurried check and closed the lights. At the rate she was falling into his arms, later might come sooner than she had planned.

Chapter Eight

"Now," Jenny announced as Brady wiped the last dish and handed her the damp dish towel. "We can talk while you help me with a school project I'm working on."

"Talk?" Taken by surprise, he stared at Jenny. No way had he expected the matter-of-fact announcement. Not after he'd seen the longing in her eyes earlier that evening.

"Yes, talk."

The determined look on her face told him she meant business. And not the kind he'd had in mind.

Brady shifted mental gears. It was difficult to do when he'd hoped for something a little more intimate than conversation. But, he reminded himself, Jenny was not only a feast for his senses, she was Max's mother. Even if the kid was adopted, she'd nurtured the boy as if she'd actually given birth to him. He owed her his thanks and his respect. Not only for the boy's sake, but also for her own, he'd go along with her. After all, he wanted her to respect him, too.

He followed her to a small den off the living room. A large, comfortable chintz couch filled one wall. A maple coffee table sat between it and a man-sized armchair. Another wall was taken up by a computer desk, computer and bookshelves lined with books. A small TV and a child-sized rocker occupied a corner, but it was obvious to Brady more reading went on in here than television watching.

The room was a riot of spring colors—yellow, green, orange and blue, with an occasional splash of lavender. He was struck by the way the room reflected Jenny's own lively, warm personality.

As inviting as the armchair looked, Brady ignored it and joined Jenny on the couch. It might be as close to her as he was going get. Too bad in a way, he thought ruefully; the scented soap bubbles dripping from her hands had sent his mind along more sensory paths. He thought of ways they might have shared the bubbles, sighed and turned his attention to Jenny's project.

She began to sort a stack of papers lying on the coffee table. Each had childish writing on it and a picture in the corner.

"Just what are we doing?" he asked curiously as he picked one up from the pile nearest him. "'*C* is for cookie,'" he read from the sheet. A short printed sentence and a picture followed, describing the author's favorite treat.

"We're working on a cookbook," Jenny explained. "It's another way to learn the alphabet and to write simple sentences. They're already in alphabetical order. Hand me Johnny's *A* and *B*, please.''

"What's all this about?" he asked. "Wasn't *I* the letter *C* star?"

"You were a shining star, all right," she said, laughing as she agreed. "It's just that it's important to show the kids how to apply the letters they learn. Your performance was visual. This exercise is to put what the kids learned into action."

Their hands touched as she reached over him to take the papers from him. Silky smooth, he thought, and not just from soap bubbles. This was one part of the exercise he *did* appreciate.

"Eventually we'll have gone through the whole alphabet and each child will get his copy of the cookbook to take home." She went on to explain the project as she collated the papers.

"Are you going to need me again?" he inquired. "I'm willing, if you are."

"Need you for what?" she retorted. "To be the Mad Scientist?"

"Any way you want me, I'm yours," Brady answered with a straight face.

Jenny sniffed her reply.

Brady's spirits picked up each time her hand brushed his. The fresh smell of soap and a touch as soft as the velvet of a rose petal sent his appreciation of Jenny up several notches. He'd never had a touchy-feely type of teacher of his own or he would have remembered school with a little more enthusiasm. Still, however the evening ended, it sure made pounding at a piece of wood with a hammer worthwhile.

"Now the paper clips, please."

Jenny busied herself clipping together eighteen neat sets of papers. When she unconsciously touched the tip of her tongue to her lips as she concentrated, Brady's thoughts rushed back to the kiss they'd shared that afternoon. As he watched the sensuous sight, he suspected no amount of conversation was going to keep his mind on cookbooks or from wanting to run his own tongue over those enticing lips. With an inward sigh, he sat back and waited for what came next.

"What would you like to talk about?" he inquired when she nodded her satisfaction and looked at him expectantly. He understood full well he was going to be the subject of the discussion. No woman as decent as Jenny was going to fall easily into unknown arms.

"You. I'd like to know a little more about you," Jenny replied evenly. "Especially if you're going to be around the school observing the children."

"That sounds fair enough. Let me assure you I'm an upstanding member of the scientific community. Aside from that, my life is not so interesting."

For a moment before she relaxed, the look in her eyes told him he was on probation. He couldn't bear the thought of losing her just yet. He mentally reviewed his squeaky-clean adult years. He'd never done anything out of the ordinary, with the exception of his donation to the sperm bank. But that was the one thing he hoped she wouldn't get around to asking.

"Maybe not interesting to you, but you have become so many different men since we met."

She studied him with a quizzical expression that sent his blood pressure soaring.

"I've wondered which one you really are."

That was a surprise. He'd never thought of himself as anyone more than a staid, serious scientist. "Where would you like me to start?"

"At the beginning," she said encouragingly. "Tell me about your parents and your uncle. Ted seems to be as close to you as a father."

"Ah, well, he actually is." Brady described his parents, and the adventurous life they led without him. "I suppose I inherited their absorbing interest in research, but theirs is for the past—mine is for the present and the future. You might say my work in the field of genetics is my excitement. The more difficult the problem, the greater the challenge."

"Gosh, you must have felt awful being left alone so much of the time. Didn't your folks ever take you along?"

The compassionate look on her face touched a chord he studiously ignored.

"Once, when I was about six years old," he said thoughtfully. "I contracted a mild case of food poisoning somewhere in the Far East and wound up in a hospital. After that, I remember I refused to eat anything my mother didn't prepare. Since she had no intention of wasting her time cooking, or on me, it didn't take long before they brought me home and enrolled me in a boarding school. I stayed there through high school, then went off to college. Somewhere along the line I became interested in the study of genetics.''

''And that's what brought you to my school to discuss genetic inheritance?''

She sounded incredulous; he didn't blame her one bit. ''That, and a small boy and his mother.'' Brady waited for her reaction. He'd told her the truth and he was ready to pay the price if he was rushing things. Not that he thought his beginning to care for her as a woman instead of a research project was premature or a secret. Most women would have caught on to him by now, but he'd already learned Jenny was unaware of her appeal.

He had plenty of free time and he couldn't think of a better way to spend some of it than in an evening with Jenny. He was as attracted to her lively spirit and intelligence as he was to her unconscious sensuality.

A warm, contented feeling rolled over Jenny. *He likes me,* she thought happily as they exchanged smiles. How satisfying it was to know he saw her as a woman and not just as a schoolteacher or a mother.

''That's flattering, I'm sure,'' she acknowledged with a slight smile of her own. ''But coming from a man who says he's been too interested in his research to think about anything else, it sounds a little strange.''

Curled up in a corner of the couch, her chin resting on her knees, she studied the smile on Brady's face. It was lopsided and rakish, yet somehow it still managed to suggest a reserved, almost shy, side to him. There was no doubt about it; it was that smile that had attracted her from the start, and it still fascinated her.

He was a paradox and a riddle, changing personalities as easily as a butterfly sheds its cocoon. He was a long way from being a butterfly, but perhaps just as elusive. Each change in him intrigued her more than the one before. But, in spite of the way he stirred her fantasies, she knew better than to get carried away. She hadn't forgotten how easily she'd been misled by a beguiling smile once before.

"After I heard your theory about nurture on television, I wanted to see it in action," he explained. "I wanted to study the children when they didn't realize what I was doing. They wouldn't have behaved naturally if they'd known what I was up to."

He gazed at her, as if deciding what to say next. And what he had to say made her soften toward him even more.

"Of course," he added at her surprised expression, "I haven't given up my original belief in the role of genetic inheritance. It's just that I've been sidetracked by special circumstances."

"Eighteen of them?" Jenny smiled. She believed he referred to the children at the center; each and every one of them was a bundle of very special circumstances as far as she was concerned. If he only knew—he was scoring *mucho* points with her.

"No. As a matter of fact, just one."

His eyes raked her in a way that made her think of warm summer nights, bare skin sliding against bare skin and lovemaking under the stars. She blinked as they traded warm glances. What was there about the man that kept her thoughts straying down dangerous paths?

Jenny swallowed hard and shifted uneasily. If she wasn't careful, he would see her rush of pleasure. He was saying things she hadn't allowed herself to think about in years. The thick protective wall she'd constructed around her heart was in danger of turning into a wall of melting jelly. Joshua couldn't have done a better job at Jericho.

She knew she'd better return to a less provocative subject or the conversation would be over before she learned what she wanted to know. "Why didn't you live with your uncle if your parents didn't have time for you?"

"I was sent to boarding school when I was seven. I spent the holidays and summers with them. Both he and my Aunt Ellie were full-time professors at the university at the time," he explained.

A quirked eyebrow told her he was aware of where her thoughts had led her and why she was so interested in his early years. After the blush that she felt sweep over her, no way could she hide her reaction to the man. She tried again. "That must have been rough on you when you were young."

When Brady shrugged, Jenny's heart went out to the little boy left behind by his parents so many years ago. No wonder the man hadn't understood the importance of tender, loving care—or "nurture," as he called it— until now.

She thought of a lonely little boy living with strangers for the greater part of his young life. Had the boarding school he'd attended been a happy place? Had anyone there understood a boy's dreams, known that a bright boy needed an extra measure of patience? Provided him with the love and attention all children required in order to grow into well-adjusted adults?

Jenny compared him with Max and the children she'd taken care of during the past eight years at the Teddy Bear Care. Unless she missed her guess, Brady had lost out on most of his childhood. Maybe that was why he was so drawn to Max and why he'd fallen in so easily with her teddy-bear fantasy. A fantasy she maintained for herself as well as for the children because sometimes it was easier to talk to stuffed bears than it was to most people.

Maybe that was why his personality and his appearance kept changing, softening as he was exposed to her world of children and teddy bears. It was also lucky he had been blessed with a strong sense of humor.

Suddenly she was glad fate, in the form of an earthquake, had brought him to the nursery-school door.

"My turn to ask the questions, or aren't you finished with the story of my life?" Brady inquired when the silence between them remained unbroken.

When she nodded, he quirked an eyebrow and settled back for his turn. It was time to learn about the woman who had attracted him and who had so unexpectedly become such an important part in his thinking. "I'll bet your life has been more interesting than mine."

"Hardly," she said with a smile. "But go ahead—ask away."

"Let's see." Brady pretended to ponder the subject. "It's not difficult to see you've led a normal life—complete with mother and father and siblings?"

Jenny agreed. "I have parents and a sister who live on the East Coast. As for growing up, there's no mystery about that. I did all the things most young girls do."

"Including getting married?" he questioned, remembering her ringless finger.

"Including getting married," she echoed with a shrug. "I fell in love and married the college star football player."

Brady glanced at her in surprise. "Somehow I didn't expect that from a levelheaded woman like you. Where is he now?"

"I'm not sure. We've been divorced for a long time. But he's probably adding to his collection of admiring women. Last I heard, he was on wife number three."

"Any children?"

"None. He never wanted any, even though I did. He couldn't stand anyone taking the spotlight away from him. That—plus a few other things—was the reason for our divorce."

"And now there's Max," he said quietly.

"And now there's Max," she echoed. Her eyes sparkled as she glanced at the small rocker in the corner.

"And, happily for me, usually there are seventeen other children."

It seemed to Brady the natural moment to delve into Max's background. He wanted to know everything about the boy. He *needed* to know.

"Remember I mentioned Max told me he was adopted, that he had two mothers?" When her attention swung back to him and a question filled her eyes, he hurried to explain. "I didn't ask him, I swear. He mentioned it when he asked me where my own mother was and I told him she was somewhere in Egypt. That's when he told me his other mother was in heaven with his father."

"It's no secret," Jenny said quietly. "My cousin asked me to take him when she was told she had cancer, with only a few months to live. I've had him since he was six months old. He's always known I chose to be his mother. He thinks that makes him someone special. And, of course, he is."

"Right on," Brady agreed as he envisioned Max seated in that small, empty rocking chair. A boy who could be his own son. "You know, I've never met anyone quite like him. What about his father?"

Jenny shrugged. "I don't know. Not that it matters anyway."

"You don't know? What kind of an answer is that?" By now, Brady's sixth sense was kicking up a storm. He felt a fine sweat cross his brow as a rising premonition swept over him. He rose and planted himself in front of her. "Max told me his father is in heaven. Surely you must have known your cousin's husband before he died!''

"Of course I knew Carl. I never said I didn't.'' She straightened. A puzzled expression passed over her face as she looked at him closely. ''He was killed in an automobile accident a month before Max was born. But he wasn't actually Max's father.''

The hairs on the back of Brady's neck started to tingle. ''Then who was?'' Even before Jenny confirmed them, he knew his suspicions about the circumstances of Max's conception were on target. He was positive he knew what she was going to say next.

''Carl and Marjorie tried to have children for several years, before they found out Carl was sterile. That's when they decided to apply to a sperm bank.''

''Which bank was that?'' He was afraid to ask if the donor's sperm had come from the Thurgood Institute, for fear his question might give him away. If Jenny connected him to the bank, he was dead. He needed time. Time to make certain he *was* Max's father, time to get Jenny to trust him. To reassure her he would never harm her or try to take Max away from her. He held his breath as he waited for the answer.

''If I ever knew, I've forgotten,'' Jenny answered. ''Not that it makes a difference. But this one came highly recommended—Marjorie made sure of that. Anyway, it took a long time to find a match, a man whose coloring and background were similar to Carl's. A donor was eventually located after a few months. Max is the happy result.''

"Artificial insemination," Brady said quietly. He dropped back onto the couch. If ever a premonition of his had come true it was now. The confirmation that Max had been born as the result of artificial insemination closed the circle of circumstance.

As far as Brady was concerned, he was closer than ever to the truth.

Pleasure, mixed with anxiety, swept over him. Shivers of excitement ran down his spine. He was a father! He was sure of it.

But what would Max's adoptive mother think if she knew that he believed *he* was Max's father? And how the devil was he going to go about proving it without frightening her off?

"You look surprised," Jenny commented, a frown creasing her forehead as she studied his strange reaction to her comments. "I don't understand why. You not only work in the field of eugenics, you were defending the practice not too long ago."

"Right." Brady shook his head in a futile effort to clear it. It wasn't every day a man became a father, even if dozens of questions remained unanswered before Brady could find out for certain. He had to get his thoughts in order, to plan what he was going to do next. Tonight was not the time.

"I guess I should call it a night," he said, reluctantly getting to his feet. "Did you find any answers to my deep secrets, or have I left you in the dark?"

Jenny grinned and rose from the couch. "For now. Perhaps we can do this again another time."

"Well, thanks for dinner. It was great. I'll see you at the school tomorrow."

"Tomorrow? Don't you ever work?" Jenny led the way to the door.

"I'm doing fieldwork, or hadn't you guessed?" The swing of her hips fascinated him; the heady, still faintly soapy scent of her tickled his senses until he wasn't certain he'd be able to walk away from her. He heard her gentle laugh.

She was only inches away from him when they reached the door. He had to fight off the desire to pull her into his arms and fulfill his promise of that afternoon.

He glanced back at the pint-sized rocker and pictured its small owner sitting there, listening to Jenny read the latest kids' story. He couldn't do anything to jeopardize his chance of bringing the boy into his life— and, if all went the way he wanted it to, maybe the kid's mother, as well.

"Now that you know all about me, I hope you're not against a good-night kiss," he asked, looking down at her sparkling blue eyes, which reminded him of clear sky after a spring storm. "For starters, anyway?"

"Not at all," she said softly, her heart beginning to race at the warmth she saw in his eyes. "I haven't heard anything about you tonight to suspect I might run into something sinister. Besides, I believe the truce we have is still in effect."

"Good. Now that we're friends, we'll have to reopen negotiations and add a few rights and privileges to that truce, won't we?" he asked as he took her in his arms and bent to kiss her welcoming lips.

Something about the way she put her arms around his neck and pressed close to him told him she had been waiting for just this moment as much as he. He kissed her tentatively at first, then gave in to his fantasy. Her lips were warm and eager as they met his. He never wanted to let her go.

He kissed each corner of her mouth, her rosy lips, slowly, thoroughly. He couldn't get enough of her. When she didn't draw away, he deepened the kiss until her lips parted and allowed him entry. She tasted of all that was good and sweet, and left him longing for more. He had to force himself to remember he had things to settle before he got in too deep. When the kiss was over, he sensed they both were sorry it had ended.

JENNY MADE HER WAY upstairs to bed, her lips still tingling from Brady's kiss. She could still feel the strength of his arms around her, his hard body against hers when he'd drawn her closer to him and the coffee taste of him when he'd deepened the kiss. A welcome tide of sensation remained with her still.

She was too aware of what he meant by "rights and privileges." Unless she'd misread the promise in his gaze, he intended to collect on them soon. An inner voice and the tingling in her body told her "soon" couldn't come soon enough.

There hadn't been another man in her life she felt she could believe in since her divorce. Certainly none whom she could entrust with her heart, she thought as she undressed and slipped into a nightgown. But did she need a man? Did she actually want one now?

Max and the nursery school had filled her life for five years. She didn't have to answer to anyone, didn't have to build up a wounded male ego. Still, the part of her that she'd deliberately kept hidden demanded more: a life partner who was capable of cherishing her as she would cherish him. Who would want children and the life-style that went with them.

Above all, a man who would be a good role model for Max.

As for her, did she for once dare hope for something for herself?

WHEN BRADY LET himself into his apartment, he found Alfred seated in a corner of the couch, waiting for him. Good, he thought as he crossed the room and picked up the stuffed brown bear. Still high from the kiss he'd shared with Jenny, Brady needed to have someone to talk to. The bear seemed to be waiting for his story. Why not? Alfred had always been a good listener.

Brady sank onto the couch, set the bear on his knee and regarded the enigmatic smile embroidered on its small brown face.

"Well, Alfred, that woman is absolutely marvelous! No wonder she has such a neat kid. Not only that, it looks as if I'm getting closer to finding out the truth about Max. I learned about his adoption today and that his father was someone who donated the sperm that was given to his birth mother. But I'll be damned if I know what to do now.''

The silence stretched on while he searched the bear's face for some clue to what he should do next. To Brady's regret, Alfred continued to smile as if to say the decision was Brady's alone.

''I wish you could talk and had all the right answers. I can't afford to do anything rash at this stage of the game, you know? Yeah, I realize I could talk it over with Ted,'' he said into the silence, ''but I'm a grown man with three advanced degrees, one of them in clinical psychology. As a matter of fact, I'm great at handing out advice to almost everyone dumb enough to ask. You'd think I'd be able to solve my own problems.''

If Jenny only knew the half of it, she'd have him tarred and feathered and thrown into the ocean, Brady mused. He leaned his head against the back of the couch and, since he didn't have a clue how to solve the riddle of whether he was Max's actual biological father, his thoughts wandered back to Jenny.

She was lovely to look at, intelligent and definitely all woman. And, incidentally, had earned much more than his respect. She was a woman who had enough love in her heart to nurture seventeen children besides her own.

Did she have enough left over for him?

He sighed and started to his feet, when he noticed a change seemed to come over Alfred's face. As if the bear had spoken out loud, Brady heard a commanding voice speak to him: *Why don't you ask her? Better do it now before it's too late. That's the only way you're going to get the answer to that question.*

By God, Alfred was right, Brady thought as he glanced at the bear and then at his wristwatch. It was almost eleven o'clock. If he was lucky, there was still time to get some answers.

He dialed the number he remembered seeing on Jenny's phone, hoping against hope that she was awake.

"Hello? Is everything okay?" a cautious voice answered.

"It's me, Brady, and yes, everything is okay. I'm sorry I'm calling so late, but I have to ask you something."

"Oh, Brady."

He heard a relieved laugh.

"Thank goodness it's only you. I was afraid something might be wrong with Max! It's the first time he's been away from home and I've been on edge for fear he might be homesick. Did you say there was something you wanted to ask me?"

"You might say so." He hesitated. How was he going to phrase a question so delicate it had taken him all this time to get up enough courage to ask it? Alfred was right. There was only one way, and it was now or never before he got cold feet.

"I haven't been able to get you out of my mind all night," he said in a rush of honesty. He had nothing to lose and everything to gain. And maybe, just maybe, he and Jenny could talk things out about Max and he could get back into her good graces. "I was wondering if you were interested in having me come back to-night?" He bit his lips as he listened to the silence at the other end of the line. Would she think him some kind of a nut for asking? Would he forfeit the friendship and the truce he'd so recently managed to strike with Jenny?

"Jenny, are you still there?" he asked into a pregnant silence. "I wanted to know if I could come back tonight."

"I thought you'd never ask."

Chapter Nine

It was the witching hour of midnight when Brady rang the doorbell to Jenny's town house. Every nerve in his body throbbed in anticipation of the moment when he could hold her in his arms and show her how he felt about her.

In his hand, he held a single red rose, which he'd stopped to purchase at an all-night market. A legend posted alongside the refrigerated case had explained the meanings of flowers. Roses were for love; a red rose for mad, passionate love; pink for friendship; and yellow for respect. He was about to choose the pink for safety's sake, when he suddenly remembered Jenny's parting words on the phone: *I thought you'd never ask.* Giving in to a sudden impulse, he'd reached for a brightly hued red rose.

From then on, all thought of hashing things out about Max seemed to evaporate from his mind.

She was a vision of loveliness when she opened the door. Her auburn hair was the fiery color of the sun as it sank below the horizon. Pink toes, looking warm and inviting, peeked from under the hem of her pink robe. At the neckline of her matching gown, he caught a glimpse of white lace and soft golden flesh. Her hair, freed from a ponytail, flowed around her high cheekbones and glowing complexion. Shy sapphire blue eyes met his.

She was everything a man dreamed of, if he had the good sense to dream at all. His own life-style and his research had kept him too busy to dream of meeting a woman like Jenny, but now things had changed. He'd put his research on the back burner after an inner voice told him he'd been waiting for just this woman to come into his life.

In the few weeks he'd known her, he'd learned she was a woman to whom passion came naturally. Passion for life, for creatures big and small. And, he thought with a tender smile, enough to spare for Alfred and his comrades. Would she have enough passion left over him?

Silently he handed her the rose.

When his hand lingered on hers, Jenny's heart began to race. The warmth of his touch coursed through her like liquid heat. There was something special about this man, she thought as his eyes caressed her. He looked at her as if he actually saw into her soul.

How had he known roses were her favorite flower and red her favorite color? And did he know how she trembled inside at the prospect of giving herself to a man for the first time in more than five years?

A warmth curled around her heart at the magic in the rose's scent and the growing desire reflected in Brady's eyes. ''Where in heaven's name did you find a rose at midnight?'' she asked as she inhaled its scent and smiled her gratitude at him over the fragrant petals.

''Where there's a will there's a way,'' he answered with a whimsical smile as he tenderly brushed her warm cheek with the back of his hand. ''I wanted to see that funny little smile you wear when you're pleased.'' He hesitated a minute before he put his hands on her shoulders, tilted her head up to his and looked into her eyes. ''I don't want you to think this is just a line, but I've thought of nothing else but being here with you for days. I didn't have the courage to ask until tonight, but Alfred made me do it,'' he said with an unsteady laugh.

''Alfred?'' she echoed, laughing, shaken by the look in his eyes. ''How could Alfred have made you call me? No matter how I pretend, he's just a teddy bear.''

''He's wiser than you realize.'' Brady lightly ran his fingers over her lush lips as he spoke. ''Just by listening, he helped me understand how much you mean to me. He made me take a good look at myself, and I wasn't too happy with the lonely man I saw. No matter that he's a stuffed bear—the little guy has me thinking straight for the first time in years. Thank you for giving him to me.''

''You're welcome,'' she whispered into his sensual eyes. ''You mean a great deal to me, too, and I didn't need Alfred to tell me so.'' The heat of him as he pressed against her penetrated her robe and turned her body into a toasted marshmallow. The arms that held her made her ache for what his voice and his eyes promised. She recognized this was something more than just a need for sex. Lord knows she'd had no trouble going without that for the past five years. She'd deliberately put the thought of love and loving out of her mind since her divorce.

But now things were different. She needed to be a part of someone, someone who cared about her. Someone who would treat her with a tenderness that made her feel valued and cared for. That she wanted to be part of this particular man came as no surprise. She'd known for days he was the man who could weave a dream around them and make it come true.

Not that Brady had mentioned love, she thought with a pang of regret. Maybe he was a man to whom expressing the emotion wouldn't come easily. Still, his gaze radiated a tenderness for her that her body craved and her mind yearned for. The idea that they could be in love and make a life together was still too new for her and, perhaps, for him. She needed time to take the idea and examine it before too much longer. Until then, she was willing to wait.

He held her so close she could feel the beat of his heart grow stronger, his body harden against hers.

"Are you sure about this, Jenny?" he whispered as he caressed her shoulders and turned her afire. "There's still time to remain just friends."

From the tight sound of his voice, she knew how hard it must be for him to offer her this last chance to change her mind. She snuggled closer to him, felt his muscular chest under her fingertips. As if she intended to change her mind!

"Is that what you really want—to remain friends? What about all those rights and privileges you mentioned?" she teased with a tender smile.

"Now that I've realized how much you mean to me, I don't want to be just friends. As for rights and privileges," he added wickedly, "maybe we can start taking advantage of them now."

She nodded slowly, letting her eyes speak for her. He should have known he already had his answer when he'd called and she'd asked him to come back. She wasn't in the habit of teasing or playing games. This was more than a game to her, but somehow she couldn't give herself to him until she was sure it was more than a game to him, too.

When his eyes darkened, she was shaken by the passion that blazed there. This was no game to him, she realized with a surge of desire. His eyes mirrored the same desire she felt coursing through her body, the same raw need. She was more than willing to follow where he led.

"You're right. Friendship isn't what I have in mind, sweet Jenny. Let me show you what we both want," he whispered into her throat as he gathered her into his arms. "Just point the way."

He took the stairs two at a time and strode with her down the short hall to her bedroom. The pink-mauve-and-lavender room, its windows framed in frothy white lace curtains, turned out to be only steps away. But to Brady, hugging Jenny to him as if he would never let her out of his arms, it felt more than a dozen miles.

Moonlight streaming through the curtains had turned the room into a fairyland. There was a large maple bed under a canopy of lace that was made for loving, he thought as he lowered her onto the bed. It was a bower fit for a fairy princess who masqueraded as a twentieth-century, jeans-clad, nursery-school teacher.

Their eyes locked as he slowly undid the sash at her waist. "We may not be making love outside under the stars, but I promise that before we're through, you'll think we are," he murmured into her luminescent eyes.

Jenny's sweet smile dared him to carry out his promise. He was a man who never could resist a challenge, he thought as he gently drew the robe from her shoulders down to her slender waist. He wanted to drown himself in her, to shout his happiness at finding a loving and honest woman not afraid to yield to her sensuality. A woman who was unconditionally giving him the most precious gift of all: herself.

Holding her gaze with his own, he carefully undid a row of tiny buttons hidden in the lace of her nightgown, one by one, stroking her soft skin. He teased her, tested her endurance, played on her sensuality until she stirred under his hands and her eyes begged for something more. She wanted him as badly as he wanted her. The pulse throbbing at the side of her neck gave her away.

She was like a dew-dropped rose under his hands, passion slowly unfolding, petal by graceful petal, as she relinquished herself to him. Under his ardent hands, her velvet skin glowed with desire. He bent to kiss her throat, the hollow between her breasts, savoring that desire on his tongue, drawing it into his very being.

Languidly, sensually, he stroked her skin, igniting carnal sparks. When she murmured her pleasure, he gave in to the impulse to taste her skin between her breasts where a small mole called to him. He bent to run his tongue over the birthmark while he unbuttoned the nightgown all the way, pushed it aside and caressed her golden breasts. She took his face in her hands and pressed him to her heated skin.

He kissed the breasts she offered, lathing each one lovingly, until her breath caught and she moaned her pleasure. The sound set him ablaze with a fire only this woman could extinguish.

"You are so beautiful, sweet Jenny," he whispered as he finally took the last of her clothing from her. "Within and without."

She'd been without a man's touch too long, Jenny thought dimly as the heat of Brady's passion swirled around her and buffeted her like a whirlwind. Desire swept over her. Her senses hovered on the brink of some unknown place that seemed to beckon to her. It was a place she'd never been before. As Brady's breath quickened and her body came alive under his hands, she gave the whole of herself into his keeping. The taste, the feel, the scent of him overwhelmed her. Heightened sensations surged around her, pulling her closer and closer to the edge of someplace wonderful and mysterious. A place she'd only dreamed of until now. With his lips on hers, coaxing her to open to him, she finally, and for the first time, felt paradise within her grasp.

The flame within her that had flickered into life at his first gentle touch grew steadily as his eyes caressed her and his sensuous hands created new sensations in her.

His gaze holding her, he sat up and shrugged out of his own clothing. When he lay down beside her and gathered her into his arms, she saw his eyes grow darker still. She felt lost in an erotic dream where his every glance, every touch created another burst of pleasure.

"Lovely Jenny," she heard him whisper, his warm breath flowing over her as lightly as a butterfly's wings stirred the air in passing.

His cheek slid against her skin, her breasts, her waist and down the outside of her thighs. Slowly he kissed his way to her toes. He tasted each one before he nipped it, then kissed it as though to apologize in case he'd hurt her, and then he moved on. Breathless, with a hunger that was building inside her until she could scarcely bear it, she felt him touch the inside of her thighs, before touching her all over and kissing his way to her lips, until she was almost mindless with passion.

His kiss was deep, his body welcome as she opened herself to him. She wanted to touch him as he'd touched her, never wanted the moment to end. As she put her arms around him and pulled him closer, she felt his muscles tense. In a burst of pleasure her own body responded to his groan of release.

Just as he'd promised, the passion that swept her filled the night with bright stars that exploded into a thousand pieces and showered her in a burst of glory.

Dimly, she was grateful it was Brady who had awakened her to the touch, the taste of a man who could be both friend and lover. A man who could show love without feeling his masculinity threatened. A man who would be there for her as she would be for him. A man who would cherish her.

He was the man and this was the moment she'd been waiting for all her life.

THE SOUND of the shower running awakened her. For a moment she was startled, until, through the dim morning light, she saw Brady's clothing neatly folded on a chair beside the bed. She smiled as she thought of his meticulous ways and how he'd stopped to straighten his clothing. They contrasted with how her own robe and nightgown had been thrown carelessly across tangled blankets.

When memories of the night just past flooded her, desire was born again. What would happen, now that they were no longer cloaked by the velvet magic of the midnight hour?

Her question was answered when Brady came into the bedroom toweling his hair and wearing only a towel around his lean waist. As they exchanged ardent glances, the first rays of dawn crept in between the frothy window curtains.

"You have a school to run and I have to leave," he said reluctantly. "There's something I have to do before I see you again," he added as he bent over her to kiss her awake. "Not that I want to, sweetheart. I'd much rather spend the day right here in heaven with you."

Heaven? Her ex-husband had seldom spoken to her after his perfunctory lovemaking, let alone referred to their moments together as heaven.

She arched upward, pulling Brady down to her. A secret smile came across her lips when his breath quickened. His scent and gaze were pure male as he held himself over her. Drops of water still clung to him. Absorbed in the clean taste of him, she ran her tongue over his damp skin and licked away a drop. When he fixed her with his sensuous eyes, her own breath quickened, her body ached for him.

"Stay," she murmured into his lips, even though she knew that men nowadays didn't necessarily make commitments. "Stay, even if only for a little while?"

With a wry groan of surrender, Brady dropped the towel behind him. He slid under the covers and gathered her to his heart. "Next time, let's make it an entire weekend," he murmured as he ran his tongue over her ear. "I need to have more time to show you how I can't seem to know enough of you."

"Show me now," Jenny whispered.

BRADY FELT like a heel. Before a night spent loving Jenny, his first priority had been to find out if Max was his son. Instead he'd found himself falling in love with the boy's mother! Somehow he felt it was all wrong; he'd gotten it backward. Until he could resolve what his relationship to Max was, he had no business making love to Jenny. He had to prove he loved her for herself, to make certain there would never be questions or doubts between them later if she learned what he was after before he told her himself. Until then, lovemaking had to be put on hold; it wouldn't be fair to her to continue this way.

He was all the more determined to find out if his sperm had fathered Max. No way could he continue, with the possibility facing him that Jenny might discover his original reason for coming to the nursery school. Heaven help them both if she decided he was using her merely to get at Max. He had to unearth the truth and tell her himself. At the right time, of course. And that time was fast approaching.

Once the issue of Max's parentage was resolved, he would pick up where he had left off last night. Any future relationship would be just between the two of them, with no questions or past ghosts coming between them.

He drove to La Jolla faster than the law allowed. On the way, he cursed the institute's tight secrecy rules and himself for his earlier indifference to the possible consequences of his donation.

If he was right, he'd helped to create a human life. He had some responsibility now that he'd discovered Max, for Pete's sake! At the time of his donation, he hadn't realized or even stopped to consider, that it could eventually come to mean more to him than a contribution to science. What had made him think his genes were any better than some other man's anyway? IQ be damned. Jenny was right.

Max's smile flashed in front of him. How could he not have wanted to see a child of his own making?

It wasn't going to be easy, but Doug *had* to be made to realize how important it was for Brady to know when his sperm donation had been used and by whom.

"No way! You damn well know I can't look into the records for you! You agreed to forget the whole thing when you made the donation." Doug shook his head adamantly. "Hell, it was at least four or five years ago, if I remember correctly. Why are you so interested in who received the sperm now, or if there even is a child? What good could possibly come of knowing the facts now?"

"That's the whole point! I think I've finally met the kid." Brady went on to tell his friend about Max, Jenny and the boy's deceased parents. "Jenny herself told me Max was conceived with sperm from a sperm bank. After being around the kid for a couple of weeks and seeing the similarity between us, I'm positive he's mine!"

"Did she say the sperm came from our bank?" Doug frowned when Brady shrugged.

"No. She just said a sperm bank was involved. How could I ask her the name without giving myself away? She might not know anyway, so I had to try you first."

"Come on, you can't be that sure it was our bank." Doug winced when Brady shot him a poisonous glare. "Even if it's the truth, and I'm not saying it is," he added hastily when Brady opened his mouth, "the lady may never find out unless you tell her."

"On the other hand, she just might," Brady retorted in frustration. "Hell, all she has to do is *see* us together often enough to know I'm his father! I've got a snapshot of myself at the kid's age that shows he's a dead ringer for me."

"It doesn't make any difference," Doug insisted as he shook his head. "I'd like to help you, Brady, but you know it's against the rules. Why don't you just let it go?"

"Damn those rules!" Brady swore as Doug continued to shake his head. "I want Jenny to be able to trust me, to believe I love her for herself and not just for her son," Brady answered as he ran his fingers through the shock of hair that kept falling over his forehead. "Jenny is the kind of woman who deserves the truth."

"The answer is still no." When Brady started to argue his case, Doug interrupted. "Tell me, what part of the word *no* don't you understand?"

"I just can't accept it as final!"

"Why don't you just lay the resemblance down to coincidence and let it go at that? Why rock the boat when, from what you say, everything seems to be going so well for this Jenny of yours and her son?''

Brady shrugged. "She's not *my* Jenny yet, but I wish she were. You may think I'm putting you on, but the truth is I think I've fallen in love with her." At Doug's sharp look, he paused. "Let me rephrase that. I am in love with her. When this is all over I'm going to ask her to marry me. Until then, I can't build our relationship on an unknown quantity that might come back to haunt me. I'd lose her in the blink of an eye. No, I have to find out the truth before I tell her what I believe to be true. I have to make her understand I love her for herself and not just for the boy."

"So, you've finally decided to join the rest of us poor suckers caught in the marriage trap?"

"Yes, if that's what you want to call it," Brady confessed with a helpless grin. "Although your Diana had better not hear you call it that if you value your life. As for me, I guess I found Jenny when I least expected it. This is one part of my life I didn't plan, order or organize."

"Should be all the more interesting." Doug nodded wisely. "Although I've known you long enough to realize that this isn't the way you like to operate. I would guess from listening to your story, my friend, you've changed in more ways than you appreciate. Maybe for the better." He grinned. "You've been a loner long enough. Some of us guys were beginning to get jealous of that freedom of yours."

Frustrated, Brady paced up and down the laboratory, finally stopping in front of one of the computers. He knew Doug worked on the program that matched donors with applicants. Unless he missed his guess, the sperm bank's records were buried somewhere in there. Maybe he could come back over the weekend and find the data for himself when no one else was around.

"I'd hate to be in your shoes, not knowing if this kid is yours or not," Doug said sympathetically, yet firmly. "But the fact remains, I couldn't help you even if I wanted to."

He caught Brady's sidelong glance at the computer on the lab table. "Forget it, my friend." He laughed. "I can tell what you're thinking. You forget I've known you too long. I can read your mind like an open book. In the first place, the computers in here are locked when I'm not around. And none of the guys who work here and who donated to the sperm bank have the password, either. I'm the only one who does."

Brady knew his goose was cooked. Given time, he probably could have come up with the password and hacked his way through the program that would reveal the truth. But with the computer locked and Doug aware of his intentions, he didn't stand a chance. Even if it killed him, he had to cool his relationship with Jenny for now. He and Jenny ought to go back to friendship while the getting there was still possible. *If* it was possible, after a night like last night.

He remembered glowing eyes, soft skin and warm embraces. Cool it? How could he, when he ached for

Jenny's loving touch? He had to! At least until he found a way to tell her of his belief that Max was his son. If he couldn't obtain the information from the computer memory, he would have to get her to allow Max's blood to be tested with his own.

As his Uncle Ted was fond of saying, Brady figured his chances of persuading her to do that were about as good as a snowball's in hell.

Chapter Ten

Jenny glanced impatiently at the clock on the school-room wall. The morning was almost gone and Brady should have been here by now. Where was he?

After the night they'd shared, she'd expected him to be on her doorstep when school opened. So why wasn't he here, today of all days?

Last night when he'd handed her the single dew-tinged red rose, the look in his eyes had stopped her in her tracks. It had been the beginning of one of the happiest nights she'd ever known.

She could still feel the consuming touch of his hands, his hard lips blazing a heated trail over her body. The impassioned look in his eyes when he'd made her his still lingered.

She'd never known a man like him before, or even dreamed of finding one until last night.

Although he hadn't once mentioned a future together, it was wonderful to think of a husband like Brady. One who, in spite of his compulsive but humorous habits, was the kind of a man who would understand and cherish her own easy ways. A man who, from what she'd seen of him around children, would be a good father to her son.

She'd be smart to take each day as it came, she reluctantly decided, glancing at the large wooden clock on the wall one more time. There was no point in rushing into a relationship. Not after she'd been on her own for so long.

She looked over to where Max was impatiently hopping on one foot. True to form, he'd waited until the last moment to use the bathroom. He was all boy and growing up fast, she once again acknowledged fondly as she saw his turn come up and he dashed inside. No longer a baby, he needed a man in his life who would be a good role model. A man who would teach him all the things a growing boy needed to know. Her heart of hearts told her Brady could be the one.

Max had been so excited after his first sleepover with Tommy when Mrs. Cooper had brought him to school this morning. He'd been invited to spend the coming weekend with them, he'd announced, and wanted to go. When Mrs. Cooper had laughingly joined in to explain her plans to take the children to the railroad park and the zoo at Griffith Park, Jenny had hesitated only for a moment before agreeing. For Max's sake and her own.

With Max away and her mind at ease, maybe she and Brady could spend the time learning more about each other, take up where they'd left off last night. And, perhaps, she thought happily, start to plan a future together.

Thank goodness for the diversion of the children, she decided as she helped them get ready for lunch. Otherwise she'd be stewing about Brady's late arrival, or if he was really going to arrive at all.

Maybe she was presuming too much. Maybe last night meant more to her than it did to him. His actions when he left had been puzzling. Especially when he'd asked her to believe in him. Could their encounter have been a one-night stand?

Just as quickly, she realized he wasn't the type. He might be late, but Brady was reliable by nature. Wasn't he?

BY THE TIME he arrived at four-thirty, she'd almost given up on him. Lunch, play and nap time had come and gone. The man-sized peanut butter-and-jelly sandwich she'd made for him was languishing in the refrigerator. All her future plans for the two of them had been scrapped, along with dreams she'd decided were premature.

Jenny was deep in story hour when he finally came in the room. Her breath caught in her throat when she saw him glance her way. All her doubts and anxieties vanished. Maybe she *had* been wrong about him.

He put his finger to his lips when he caught her eye, then skirted the rug and seated himself at the back of the room. A smile teased his lips as nodded to Max before turning his attention to another story about Curious George, the monkey whose curiosity inevitably led him into trouble. She settled her reading glasses more firmly on her nose. With a brief answering smile of her own, she continued reading.

Out of the corner of her eye, she saw Max inch his way backward until he sat alongside Brady's knee. Her heart went into instant meltdown when Brady bent over to gently rumple Max's hair and whisper in his ear. They grinned into each other's eyes, and for the first time, she realized how much alike they really were.

A lovable child, her son made friendships easily. But none had come so swiftly as the bond he'd formed with Brady. From the way Brady treated Max, she could tell the feeling was mutual. Maybe because the boy was hers?

It was amusing to see how Max kept his eyes fixed on Brady, shifting when Brady moved, smiling when Brady smiled. He had begun to imitate Brady's walk, his mannerisms. Even to the way he kept brushing his hair out of his eyes. If Brady had a fan club, Max would be his number one fan.

Jenny tried to pull her thoughts together, to concentrate on Curious George's latest escapade. At the point where George became tangled up in a tablecloth and fell down a flight of stairs right into the middle of a Halloween costume party, Brady's lips parted in a big grin, just like the children's. If the story was old hat to her, it was evidently new and interesting to him.

It was a good thing she could recite the dog-eared storybook by heart, she reflected with an inward sigh. It was Brady who had her attention. She caught herself looking at his hands and remembering their touch, the taste of his lips, the lingering throb of his heart against hers. With a jolt, she came back to Curious George, hoping no one noticed that her breath had caught in her throat.

Story hour over, Max jumped up and bounded toward her. "Mommy, Mr. Morgan wants to know if we can go shopping on the way home."

"Shopping? What kind of shopping?" Jenny's gaze met Brady's. How could he appear so cool and innocent behind that amicable smile? If he remembered last night as vividly as she did, he sure wasn't showing it. The casual, friendly look on his face disturbed her. Was it only because Max clung to his hand that he gave no hint that he remembered last night? Or had she wanted Brady so badly she'd read too much meaning into their encounter?

How could he not remember a night she couldn't forget?

Hiding the sudden ache that gripped her heart, she put her reading glasses in her shirt pocket and casually returned his smile. If she had anything to say about it they were going to talk as soon as they had some privacy. As soon as she settled Max's weekend, she'd take care of her own.

"I hope you don't intend to shop for toys," she cautioned, ignoring the look of dismay on her son's face. Trips to toy stores usually wound up in hurt feelings and were a financial disaster. "If you're not careful, Max will have you visiting every toy store in the county!"

"Not exactly." Brady glanced down at an indignant Max and swallowed a grin before he explained. "You may not believe this, but there's something better than the run-of-the-mill toy stores, sport. When I was young, my own toys came from a hardware store."

Max appeared doubtful.

"A hardware store! You have to be putting us on." Jenny thought of nuts, screws, bolts and washers and maybe a hammer or two. But toys? "What kind of toys can you find in a hardware store?"

"You'd be surprised," he assured her with a conspiratorial side glance at a wide-eyed Max. "My Uncle Ted introduced me to hardware stores early on, and I've never gotten over the excitement of those first visits. That was when I got my first carving knife and a chunk of balsa wood for a birthday present."

"A knife? Can I have a real knife?" Max interrupted breathlessly.

"You're too young for knives!" Jenny reached for Max and pulled him to her side. "No way!"

"But, Mommy, I have to have a knife so I can make you a present, just like the wooden bear Mr. Morgan made for you!"

"Max! I said there will be no knives." Jenny sternly eyed her son, then trained her attention on Brady. "No knives," she repeated when Max tried to pull away.

"Men don't have temper tantrums," Brady admonished Max quietly. "You mother is right."

"But I'm not a man," Max protested. "I'm just a little boy, and I want to be cool just like you, Mr. Morgan."

"Well, you want to grow up to be a man, eventually, don't you?" Brady rejoined.

"Sure I do! I want to grow up to be just like you!"

"Then you'd better listen to your mother," Brady advised with an embarrassed grin at Jenny. "She'll show you how."

Annoyed at being left out of the conversation, Jenny placed both hands on her son's shoulders. "Maybe it's not a good idea for you to go off with Mr. Morgan after all."

"The point is," Brady interjected when Max started to protest, "Max has to learn a few rules about growing up. Just like the rules on behavior you have on the bulletin board inside. Give me a chance with the boy, Jenny. I know what I'm doing."

The quiet authority in his voice and the plea in his gaze gave her pause. "I'm not so sure about that," she said reluctantly. "You haven't been around kids all that much." When she saw tears come into Max's eyes, she unwillingly gave in. "Okay, but in any case, remember I'm dead set against knives."

"Right! Ted taught me to carve my first wooden animals," Brady explained. "I felt like a magician, taking a piece of wood, carving and painting it, bringing it to life. As a matter of fact, I still feel the same way. So I know how Max feels." He smiled fondly down at the boy. "But he can wait awhile for that. In the meantime, I'm willing to bet he'll find plenty of things in hardware stores that are more fun than any toys. Right, Max?''

Max looked dubious. He glanced up at Brady and appeared to consider the matter carefully before he reluctantly nodded. "If you say so, Mr. Morgan."

Brady nodded his encouragement. "I do. You'll find lots of things you'll like, I promise. And I always keep my promises. But no knives, not yet."

Jenny recalled a promise of another kind he'd made last night. He'd delivered on that one, exquisitely, but it didn't look as if he remembered it today. Did he still intend to deliver on the other promises she'd heard in his voice and seen in his eyes when he'd made love to her?

She pulled herself together. There was no use thinking about herself right now. Brady and Max were waiting for her answer.

"Then it's okay with me," she agreed, although from the mixture of curiosity and reluctance on Max's face he would have preferred the local toy store. After hearing the mention of tools and knives, she would have preferred it herself. Hesitantly she continued. "Max would enjoy going along with you. Exactly what were you looking for?"

"I have to pick up a few things my uncle and I will need for the weekend." When she looked surprised, he explained, "We were planning on putting together a playhouse for the kids on Saturday. Ted is taking care of arranging for the delivery of the prefab sections and

I'm going to pick up the hardware and the paint. Max could be a great help to me.''

Max's face lit up as he listened. He edged closer to Brady and turned his golden brown eyes on him.

Suddenly she realized her baby had become a boy overnight and needed more than his mother. There was a new world out there waiting to be discovered and he couldn't wait to get started. That was why she'd let him sleep over at Tommy's and why she'd agreed to let him spend the weekend with Tommy and his parents. He needed male companionship and male pursuits. Jenny knew she would have to let him grow up. She'd have to allow Brady into Max's sheltered life just as she'd allowed Brady into hers.

All of a sudden what Brady had said registered. *"Build a playhouse this weekend?"*

"Yes, why not?" Brady questioned, clearly taken aback by her reaction. "Ted and I wanted to put one up this Saturday when the playground was clear of children. That way, no one will get hurt.''

"I can't possibly pay for a playhouse right now," she protested, angry that this conversation was being carried on while Max listened. "The school needs a lot more important things than a playhouse. You should have asked me before you made any plans!''

"I don't want any money, Jenny. Let's just say it's part of my payment to you for letting me study the children. As for Ted, he can't wait to get a hammer in his hands again.''

"That's not the point!"

"Then I don't get it." Obviously frustrated, Brady raked his hair with his fingers. "I don't understand what the problem is!"

"Mommy, I think a playhouse is a good idea," Max interjected. "We could have lots of fun!"

Jenny tried to calm down, but it was difficult with Brady eyeing her. He was right, the problem was not with the proposed playhouse—it was with her. "Max, I'd like you to go back inside while I talk to Brady."

"I don't want to," he answered stubbornly. "I want to stay with Mr. Morgan."

Jenny fixed Brady with a look guaranteed to freeze a lesser man. "Now see what you've done?"

"You can't protect Max from reality, Jenny. Listening to a little friendly argument won't hurt him."

With Max avidly following their conversation, Jenny had no choice but to give in. But as soon as she could persuade Max to go inside, she'd pay Brady back, and she wasn't thinking about money. She swallowed hard. "Well, if you put it that way, I guess it's okay. The point is, in the future I'd like to be consulted before you make any plans concerning the school."

"Great," Brady said with a smile of relief as Max started to whoop his delight. "I was looking really forward to putting one together for the kids."

Jenny was looking forward to something else. "But does the playhouse project have to be this weekend?"

"Now seemed like a good time to me." Frowning, Brady asked her, "It is, isn't it?"

How could she tell him her own plans had been so very different from his? After she'd accepted the invitation for Max to spend the weekend with Tommy, she'd spent the morning envisioning a romantic rendezvous for herself and Brady. She'd planned to cash in on a prize she'd won in a charity raffle—a weekend at a luxurious hotel down the Pacific Coast in the picturesque artists' colony of Laguna Beach.

In the literature that came with the prize, the hotel shown was a two-storied Cape Cod–type property perched high on a cliff overlooking the Pacific Ocean. Balconies open to the sea seemed to have been designed for watching moonlight reflect on rolling waves breaking onshore below the hotel. There were informal English gardens; tide pools to explore; wet sand for quiet, barefoot midnight strolls. According to the brochures, it was a perfect hideaway for lovers.

Just like a man, she thought sourly as her plans evaporated. *He* was planning to spend the two days playing carpenter, while *she* was daydreaming over a romantic weekend!

She studied the two pairs of identical eyes waiting for her answer. Max knew how to turn on his melting brandy-colored eyes to charm her; he'd been doing it since he was born. From the looks of things, Brady had caught on quickly enough, too. Maybe it was a trick inherent in male genes, one guaranteed to melt a woman's heart. In which case, she decided, she might as well give in. She didn't stand a fighting chance against two pros.

"Well, I guess it would be okay, and yes, Max can go with you," she said, inwardly chiding herself for setting herself up for disappointment. She was grown-up; what she wanted wasn't settled as easily as a trip to a hardware store. She should have known better than to plan something without consulting Brady. Just as she'd expected him to consult her. It wasn't all his fault. She'd had no business taking him for granted.

Maybe men were all alike after all.

How foolish she'd been, dreaming dreams whose fulfillment was out of her reach.

"We won't be long," Brady assured her. "I'll bring Max home in about an hour."

"Okay," she answered with a meaningful look at her son. "Behave yourself and don't ask for the moon, sweetheart. I'll go on home and pick up a pizza for dinner."

Max fidgeted, tugged at Brady's hand and pulled him toward the front door. "We'd better hurry before all the good stuff is gone!"

"Not to worry," Brady said as he gestured helplessly to Jenny. "We're going to go to Home Depot. They never run out. And if they do, they'll give us a rain check."

"What's a rain check, Mr. Morgan?"

"A promise to let you have what you wanted at some other time."

Was there a message in Brady's eyes as he and Max waved goodbye, or was it something she wanted to see?

What was it about the best-laid plans...?

"OKAY, NOW HERE'S our plan of attack," Brady announced as he and Max came into the cavernous hardware store. "We'll do this thing systematically. First, the bigger items go into the bottom of the shopping cart. Then we'll fill those little plastic bags with the nails and latches we'll need for the playhouse and put them on top. The paint will go in the bottom of the cart. Got that?"

Max nodded as he gazed in awe at the endless supply of items for sale. "Sure, but where do they keep the toys?"

"Right here," Brady said as he steered Max over to a display of hand tools. "First, you'd better pick out a red toolbox from that stack over there. Find one just like mine, but make sure it's your size," he cautioned. "You'll want to be able to handle it easily."

He watched Max select a midsized box. "Maybe a smaller one for starters, sport," he suggested. "Remember, you're going to have to carry it all by yourself. Make sure it won't be too heavy." He pointed to a small red box. "Try that one on for size."

Max solemnly hefted the box. "This one feels good."

Brady swallowed a smile. "And now," he said, remembering his first shopping trip with his uncle, "how about some tools?"

"Real tools?" Max's eyes grew wide. "You mean tools that really work?"

"Real tools," Brady assured him. "Like that small hammer over there. And that little set of screwdrivers. Oh, yes, how about pliers and a few clamps?" Amused, he watched Max pick up the tools and carefully put them into his new toolbox.

"Gosh, Mr. Morgan, I don't think Mommy is going to like me having real tools," Max said in a doubtful voice. "She says I have to know the safety rules before I'm allowed to touch them. But she forgot to tell me what the rules are." He looked up at Brady, his small forehead creased with anxiety.

"No problem, sport. You're going to have to pass my Uncle Ted's safety test before you'll be allowed to use the tools anyway. Just as he made me do. But don't worry, I'll help you with them when the time comes. You look smart enough to learn them quickly enough." Brady pretended to consider the shelves for a moment. "Here, this hat ought to help keep you out of trouble."

Brady lifted the smallest hard hat he could find off a shelf and set it on Max's head. Max's eyes lit up. Brady studied the effect. Only the boy's nose and chin were left showing. Brady grinned. He picked up a blue bandanna, took the hat off Max's head and padded the inside before he put it back on. "There, now you're in business! Go check yourself out in that mirror over there."

He was amused to see Max grow in stature as he surveyed himself in a mirrored door and a wide smile came over his little face. After Max had adjusted the hat to his satisfaction, he tramped back to Brady.

"Cool, Mr. Morgan."

"So, do you like my kind of toys?" Brady asked, tongue in cheek.

"You bet! Only we forgot something."

"We did?" Brady made a show of looking around. "Just what else did you have in mind?"

"A little carving knife just like the one you have. I want to learn to carve animals just the way you do." His brown eyes twinkled.

Brady wasn't fooled. "You'll to wait a few more years before you get a carving knife. Your fingers are still too small to get a good grip on the handle. Besides, didn't we promise your mother we wouldn't buy one?" He took in the crestfallen look on Max's face, but he didn't blame the kid for trying. It was just the sort of thing he would have done himself. "I'll show you how to use one when you're ready," he assured Max as he added sandpaper to the toolbox. "In fact, I'm going to show you how to do a lot of things."

"Promise, Mr. Morgan?"

"If I have anything to say about it, I will." When the happy smile came back onto Max's face, Brady had to swallow the lump in his throat. Fatherhood was a weighty commitment, he decided as he exchanged smiles with Max. There were things to learn about children he'd never thought of before now and things he had to learn about himself, too, now that his own world was changing.

As for Max, there was so much to share with a son, so many promises to keep. And the most important one of all was the promise he'd made to himself. To be a good father to Max, to share his world, help him grow to manhood and protect him along the way.

Damn! Brady mentally cursed the position he was in. He would have liked to share a romantic weekend with Jenny, but it was more important right now to be a friend and a father. He *had* to prove he was Max's biological father in order to have the right to be there to fulfill those promises. At the rate he was going, and without any notable success so far, he didn't have a prayer. But that didn't mean he would stop praying.

And then there was Jenny. Her eyes had been filled with unsaid questions. Not that he blamed her. He'd come on like a house on fire last night, and even though that fire was still burning inside him, he had things to do before he could ask her to share its warmth.

He hoped she had the patience and the understanding to wait until he could tell her the whole story. Telling her wasn't going to be easy. Did he have what it would take to figure out a way not to break her heart in the process?

"AREN'T YOU STAYING for pizza, Brady?" Jenny stood in the doorway, shushing Max, who was trying to tell her about his adventures at the hardware store.

"Well . . ." Brady hesitated. He needed at least another few days to figure out how he was going to get at the truth without spooking her. If he came inside now, all his good intentions would probably go to hell. "Ted and I wanted to get an early start on the playhouse in the morning."

"And having pizza with us tonight would keep you from it?" She had tried to, but couldn't, keep the edge out of her voice. If last night had been heaven, tonight was hell.

"Jenny," he said, visibly disturbed for the first time that day. "Please bear with me for now. I've got a lot on my mind. There's something I need to take care of before—"

"Go on in the house, Max, and wash your hands," Jenny ordered when she saw the anguish on Brady's face. Something was wrong and she had an uneasy feeling she was part of the problem. "I'll be there in a minute."

"But, Mommy, I want to show you what Mr. Morgan bought me!"

"Go on in, sweetheart," she repeated. "I'll be in as soon as I say good-night to Mr. Morgan." This might not be the right time or the right place to tackle Brady, but she couldn't let another hour go by without doing something to soothe the growing uneasiness she felt. How could she have misread Brady's intentions? Why did she still want to believe in him?

Brady leaned over to give Max a pat on his little rear to get him started. "Go on in, sport. Your mother won't be long."

"You won't forget your promises, will you, Mr. Morgan?" Max reluctantly backed through the doorway to the town house.

"Never," Brady assured him. "I'll see you tomorrow."

Jenny waited until Max disappeared inside before she turned back to Brady. "What was that all about?"

"I promised to help him with some safety rules on handling the new tools I bought him."

"You bought him real tools when you know how I feel about that?"

"Just small ones," he explained when he saw her outrage. "Not to worry. He can't really hurt himself with them. Ted and I will be there to show him how to use them safely."

"See here, Brady, you've gone too far. You seem to have forgotten Max is only four years old." Jenny forgot her own unhappiness in her need to protect her son.

"He's smart for his age. He'll learn fast," Brady protested. "In fact, I don't think kids come any smarter. Besides, if I don't show him how to use small tools safely now, he'll only get into trouble with big tools later on."

Suddenly suspicious, Jenny studied Brady for a long moment. "What's going on here? For a man who's never had children and hasn't been around them for any length of time, why are you so interested in Max?"

Brady cursed the luck that had brought him to this point so soon. He was a fairly intelligent guy in a profession that took brains to seek out nature's secrets. Although why he hadn't been smart enough to stay out of Jenny's enticing arms until he'd determined who Max's father was beat the hell out of him.

He didn't want to hurt her, but he couldn't begin to tell her the whole truth, either. He couldn't tell her why he'd acted like a lovesick guy one night and a friend the next. He couldn't tell her how difficult it was for him to ignore how much he wanted to hold her, explore every inch of her again and again. That he wanted to see passion flare in her eyes, see her unfold in his arms like the petals of a rose.

Her eyes searched his for answers. "What is it that you aren't telling me?"

She was no fool, this lady of his. Somehow she'd sensed he was hiding something from her. How right she was!

"Jenny, I..." He reached for her before he hesitated, then dropped his arms. He saw the doubt in her eyes grow until she silently turned away. He stood speechless when she slowly closed the door behind her, taking part of him with her.

With a mixture of exhilaration and fear, he realized how close he'd come to happiness. Jenny had to be his. And Max, his son. Then he shuddered as dread entered his mind. If he lost them, it would be the greatest sorrow of his life.

He wanted to touch her, hold her in his arms, see the doubt in her gaze turn into a smile. He wanted to tell her how she and Max had wound themselves around his heart and changed his life forever. After tonight she'd never believe him.

He loved her, wanted to make her a part of his life forever. For now, however, he had no choice but to solve the riddle of Max's parentage. There was no other way out.

Chapter Eleven

If it wasn't for Max, she would have told Brady to take his so-called scientific research elsewhere and never come back.

If she hadn't desperately wanted to believe Brady had a good reason for shutting her out, she would have called him this morning and told him the school didn't need a playhouse and she didn't need him, either.

That is, if she hadn't already fallen in love with him.

Fallen in love with a man she no longer pretended to understand. A man who made her body come alive every time his eyes brushed over her, but whose body language sent signals that seemed to have changed overnight.

The one thing that hadn't seemed to change was his growing fondness for her son. He was a man who'd shown up out of nowhere and was taking over her life. The realization was strange and troubling.

The sound of a truck turning into the driveway attracted her attention. Through the schoolhouse window, she saw a rented utility van pull up and stop alongside the playground gate. Three loud blasts of its horn announced its arrival.

Moments later, Ted and Brady climbed down. They spoke briefly before Brady nodded and went around to the rear of the truck and slid open the back panel. He said something over his shoulder to his uncle, jumped into the truck and began handing down sections of wooden panels.

One large section was a precut door. Several panels had openings cut for windows. A door and the finished windows followed. Ted stacked them by the gate.

The playhouse! She'd almost forgotten Brady and his uncle intended to build one for her school this weekend.

A quick look around reassured Jenny no one else besides her and Max were paying attention to what was going on. Max was always the first to finish his daily projects, the first to tidy up his papers and his crayons without being asked—and the first to find trouble if trouble hadn't already found him. His emerging dual personality, now that he was growing older, kept her on her toes, just like someone else she knew.

Why was it that every time she saw Max and noted his meticulous ways she thought of Brady?

Their foreheads creased in concentration, the children were happily coloring the letter *D* in their alphabet diaries. If they'd known what was going a few feet from them, they would have been falling over themselves in a stampede for the door.

She motioned Cindy to open the gate, closed her eyes and wearily rested her chin in her hand. How could she look Brady in the eye after last night? And how could he go through with his plans this morning as if nothing unusual had happened?

Long after she'd closed the door last night, she'd remained standing there with her forehead against it. Instinct had told her she'd done more than just close a door. She'd closed off the trust she'd placed in a man she should never have allowed into her life in the first place.

If Brady had only told her what he was hiding from her, had explained when she'd asked him why he appeared to have changed, she would have tried to understand. Without a word of explanation, she'd only been able to think of the worst possible scenario. That she'd somehow failed him or, in spite of the rose and the rapture that had followed well into the dawn, that he hadn't really wanted her for more than one night after all.

How could she have given herself to him so easily? How could she have forgotten the heartbreak of her earlier empty marriage, which hadn't been a real marriage after all? How could she have been so wrong about him?

Her gaze fell on the little brown teddy bear lying on the edge of a chair near her. Matilda. Not really a teddy bear at all, but a friend, a confidante. The poor dear looked as if she'd been through a rough day, too.

Jenny reached to reattach the tiny red hair ribbons that were falling off the bear's ears, to straighten the minuscule skirt. "We girls have to stick together," she said as she retied the ribbons. "Some days are worse than others, aren't they? You with the kids, me with Brady."

The stuffed bear steadily returned her gaze. If Jenny hadn't known better, she would have sworn a compassionate look came over Matilda's small stitched face.

"I hate to admit it, Matilda," Jenny went on to confess to the only one she felt she could confide in, "but I'm knee-deep in man trouble. I should have listened to you and Alfred the first time Brady showed up. I should have taken it a little slower, gotten to know him before I let myself become carried away by that lopsided smile of his. It looks as if I've fallen in love with the wrong man again," she said sadly.

She regarded the listening bear with a rueful smile. "You turned out to be right, you know. You've probably heard it said many times and I'll be the first to tell you it's true. We women don't seem to be able to live with men or without them."

Jenny gazed out the window in time to see the object of her unhappiness helping his uncle carry sections of the playhouse into the storage shed.

She glanced at her watch. It was almost eleven o'clock. In twenty minutes, the children were scheduled to put on their jackets and head outside for some exercise before lunch and nap time. Brady and his uncle had better hurry before they were found out.

"Mommy," Max said in a stage whisper as he came to her side. "Both Mr. Morgans are outside."

"I know they are, sweetheart. I was just going out to see if they need some help before recess." She scrambled to her feet to warn Brady and his uncle time for secrecy was running out.

"I'll come with you," Max announced, his little body quivering in his excitement. "I have my toolbox and I'm ready to help, too."

He held up the toolbox he'd insisted on bringing to school that morning. As long as Brady was around to influence him, Jenny had no doubt Max would insist on bringing it to school every day.

"I don't think you'd better." Jenny glanced over his head to see if they were being overheard by the other children. "Mr. Morgan and his uncle wanted the playhouse to be a big surprise for everyone on Monday morning."

"He didn't mean me," Max said earnestly. "He said I was smart enough to help!"

"Well . . ." Jenny hesitated. She tried to resist the appeal in Max's eyes and failed. Since he was going to be gone for the weekend, maybe she could let him outside for a little while. "Did you finish coloring in your alphabet diary?"

"Sure! Hurry up, Mommy, before we're too late."

Max tugged at her hand and pulled her to the door. Grabbing their jackets from wooden pegs by the back door, Jenny followed him outside to where Brady and his uncle were still hard at work unloading the precut playhouse sections into the storage shed.

"Hi, sport!" Brady stood a panel against the shed, bent over and caught Max up in his arms. He laughed at the fervent hug the boy gave him, but his smile slowly faded when he saw the look in Jenny's eyes as she followed Max. They exchanged cautious glances. "After what you said yesterday about not wanting a playhouse, I hope you don't mind our coming here this morning," he apologized. "It was too late to call the whole thing off."

"Not as long as you've gotten this far," she replied, too proud to tell him how her heart ached each time she saw him and how puzzled she was over his odd behavior last night. If he wanted to behave as if the past two days had never happened, she could hide her own emotions. Until the playhouse was finished. After that, she'd give him his walking papers. In time, she'd put him out of her mind and her life, just as she had her ex-husband.

"Hi, Jenny!" Ted Morgan emerged from the shed. It was a cool February morning, but he was wiping sweat from his forehead. "Maybe I'm getting too old for this sort of thing," he said with a rueful smile. "It's a good thing Brady and Max are here to help."

"See, Mommy, I told you they wanted me to help build the playhouse!"

As she bundled Max into his jacket, Ted seemed to notice the expression on her face.

"Everything okay, Jenny?"

"Just fine," she answered, forcing a smile to her lips. "Just fine." No way was she going to let Ted know she wasn't too happy about his presence here today. He was innocent of any wrongdoing, except perhaps for looking like an older version of his nephew.

"I'm here, too, Mr. Morgan!" Max tugged at Ted's trousers. "See, I even have my toolbox ready so I can help you!"

"You don't say? Here, let's take a look at that box while I rest a bit." Ted sat down on a bench, Max at his knees. Together they opened the lid of the red box and solemnly inspected the contents.

"Do I have everything I need?" Max asked anxiously. "Mr. Morgan will get it for me if I don't. He promised."

"Well..." Ted appeared to study the neatly arranged box. "You could use a ruler and a pencil so you can make exact measurements. Wait a minute, my boy." He glanced over to where Brady was still standing by the truck. "Brady, hand me that old folding ruler I have in my toolbox. It's over there in back of the cab."

"You shouldn't give away your tools, Ted," Jenny protested. "Max has enough without them."

"But, Mommy, I want the ruler!"

"It's just an old wooden ruler I've kept around for a keepsake, Jenny," Ted said when Max started to complain. "Hold up there, son. It's yours only if your mother says it's okay."

"If you really want him to have it, it's okay," Jenny agreed. Max's face lit up. What was this hold Ted and Brady had over Max? she wondered. They could quiet him with a look or a word or two.

Jenny's attention was caught by the sight of Brady leaning into the truck cab. Solid, long legs were sheathed in worn blue jeans, and a red flannel shirt hung over the same lean hips that had slid so sensuously over hers a short two nights ago. A warmth ran through her now as she remembered the strong arms that had held her, the tender lips that had kissed her. And a red rose that had begun a night she would never forget.

Suddenly, all her attempts to forget the night they'd shared went down the tubes. With a hunger that recaptured her body and her mind, she wanted Brady to hold her, run his hands over her body, taste her lips, make her his again.

She heard the sounds of metal striking metal. There was a muffled exclamation and Brady backed out of the truck. In one hand he held a worn wooden folding ruler. As he walked over to where his uncle and Max were waiting, he sucked on the thumb of his other hand. Unless she missed her guess, he'd banged it again.

Even if the man was a fairly competent carpenter, he was mighty careless with his thumb, Jenny decided with a wry smile. And he was a hard man to stay angry with. She remembered a torn cuticle, teddy bear Band-Aids and a man who'd played at being injured to get her attention and sympathy.

He'd gotten her attention, all right, and a good deal more of her besides. She'd given him her trust and her heart during that one passion-filled night. A night she'd believed was the beginning of a special relationship.

How could he have taken them only to throw them away?

Her eyes followed Brady back to the shed. Soon she saw three heads solemnly bent over the old-fashioned ruler and the contents of Max's small red toolbox. Three heads, two of them shining golden brown under the sun, the third shot with gray, but identical forelocks covering identical brandy-colored eyes.

Jenny caught her breath. The answer to what had nagged at her suddenly became crystal clear. To her growing alarm, a portrait of three generations of Morgan males swam in front of her eyes as surely as if an artist had painted it there.

Answers to bits and pieces of a puzzle that had lingered in the back of her mind fell into place. Unanswered questions about similar eyes, smiles, even a similar walk, were answered for her now. The resemblance between the three was too great to be mere coincidence!

Brady may have come to the schoolhouse after he'd seen her and Max being interviewed on television, just as he'd said. What he hadn't told her was that it was after he'd decided he was somehow related to Max!

Related to Max? Impossible!

Frozen with disbelief, she couldn't tear her eyes from the trio. There must be a million-to-one chance that her suspicions were on target, and yet... How could she deny what her eyes were seeing and what her heart was telling her? By a quirk of fate, Max's biological father had found him.

She gasped as the reality of the situation closed in on her. The truth was right there in front of her, and had been right along. She'd just been too emotionally involved with Brady to see it.

Her thoughts in a turmoil, she remembered that Max had told Brady he'd been adopted and that his mother was in heaven. When Brady had inquired about Max's father, Jenny had told him the truth: that Max had been conceived with sperm obtained from a sperm bank.

The clues had all been there.

Brady had to believe he was Max's biological father!

Cold arrows of apprehension shot through her as she studied the engrossed trio. If before she'd dismissed the resemblance between Max and Brady as only coincidental, now she was sure it was much more than that. Brady intended to take Max away from her!

What kind of woman was she that she'd allowed her desire for Brady to get in the way of her common sense?

Fear for her son chased away the sensual thoughts and hurt feelings that had troubled her all morning.

She saw Brady glance up at her with a welcoming smile. The smile faded and slowly turned into a frown when he saw the way she stood glued to the spot, staring at them. He started to come to his feet.

Before he could move, she backed away from the scene that was beginning to terrify her. Holding her hand over her mouth to keep from blurting out her fears, she ran into her office as if the devil were hard at her heels. She'd been right, she thought wildly as she tried to quiet her pounding heart. Max *was* what had brought Brady to the school, not that scientific gibberish he'd given as his excuse.

Worse yet, he *had* to have been using her to get to Max. She understood it all now. She meant nothing to Brady. She'd only been a means to get at her son. She had to stop Brady. Now, before it was too late!

"Jenny? Is something wrong?"

Brady stood in the doorway to her office. She glanced up at him through pain-filled eyes. "You bet!" she managed as soon as she could speak. Even before she had a chance to accuse him of subterfuge, she saw the truth written on his face. He already knew he, his uncle and Max were related.

"How could you?" she asked, fighting down the urge to shout her anguish at him. Only the presence of the children outside her door kept her voice barely above a whisper. "How could you do this to me?"

"Do what, Jenny?" he said cautiously, edging his way into the office. "Just what is it you think I've done?"

"You're a fraud, Brady Morgan. A liar and a cheat!" She leaned across the desk, fixing him with all the fire and anguish welling up inside her. She wanted to beat his chest, tear out his hair, anything to hurt him as badly as he'd hurt her.

"You came here with stories any woman with an ounce of brains in her head should have known were excuses to hide the truth! But not me, gullible me, not when you were busy romancing me to keep me from seeing the truth and realizing what you're up to."

Brady sank into a chair. A deep sadness came over his face as he shrugged helplessly and met her eyes. "They weren't excuses, Jenny. After seeing you on television, I did want to talk to you about your theories on raising children. As for your son, I admit I wanted to meet him, too."

She had to give him credit for not trying to pretend he didn't know what she was talking about. "What about Max? Just what did you think you were going to do about him after you saw him?"

"At first, I only wanted to meet him, to see for myself if the resemblance between us was as strong as I thought. No more than that, I swear." He clenched and unclenched his hands as he spoke. His knuckles whitened with his tension.

"And now?" He wasn't going to get any sympathy from her.

"I know Max is my son."

"No," she cried as her fears were realized. "You're mistaken!"

She saw moisture glisten in his eyes, but she didn't care. She was being torn to pieces; if Brady was suffering, he'd brought it on himself.

"I'm sorry you had to find out this way, Jenny. I was afraid you would see the resemblance between the three of us before I had a chance to tell you myself. I wanted to be able to prove our relationship before I did. That was why I'd decided to cool it after our night together. A little late, perhaps," he apologized, "but at the time

I couldn't resist holding you, making love to you. I wanted you, if only for one night."

"For only one night! How can you cheapen what I thought was special? That you cared for me."

"I do," he answered as a bleak look came over his face. "Please believe I wanted to be able to tell you the whole truth. My motives after that night were honorable. I didn't want to use you, as you put it." When she remained unmoved, he bit his lips and rose to pace the floor. "I don't know what more I can say to make you understand how I felt. Now that you've found out, what do you plan on doing about it?"

"You tell me, *Mr. Morgan,*" she said bitterly, glancing at Max's framed photograph and back to Brady. "How do I go about breaking a little boy's heart?"

"By giving him a father? What could be more right than that? It's what I wanted more than anything in the world when I was young." He reached across the desk beseechingly. "Jenny, a boy needs his father. And I need my son."

"You do know how to trade on innocence, don't you?" Jenny said, surging to her feet. "It won't work. Get out of my office and get out of my life. After today, I never want to see you again!"

He stood there, gazing at her. He started to speak, then stopped. She could see he wasn't ready to accept her decision as final, but she didn't want any part of him. At her continued silence, he studied her for a moment, before he turned and left.

WHEN THE DOORBELL of her town house rang that night after she'd tucked Max in bed, she was sure it was Brady. She flung open the door ready to tell him again that she didn't want any part of him.

Her visitor was Ted Morgan.

"I hope you don't mind my coming here tonight, Jenny, but I had to talk to you." He briefly glanced around the room before he turned back to her. "I waited until I thought Max would be asleep so we could talk without upsetting him."

She held the door open and gestured for him to come in. "If you came here to talk for Brady, you're wasting your time," she told him. "But as long as you're here, you can come in."

"Brady told me about the confrontation you had this morning," he explained as she led the way into the den and motioned for him to take the couch. "Forgive me for getting involved in all this, Jenny. It's only because I love Brady as if he were my own son that I wanted you to understand his motives for wanting to be a father now that he's found Max. As for Max, I confess I've grown quite fond of the boy in the short time I've known him. And you, too, my dear. If I could, I'd like to keep this from getting out of control."

"There's nothing left to talk about. No matter who Brady thinks he is, I want him out of Max's and my life!" She wiped tears from the corners of her eyes with the back of her hand and sank down on the couch beside him. "But then, you're not responsible for your nephew's actions, are you?"

"So you'll forgive me for coming here tonight?" he asked.

"There's nothing to forgive," she answered, hardening her heart against the soft twinkle in his eyes and the same killer smile that he shared with his nephew and Max. "Brady is your nephew—you're bound to defend him. Max is my son—I have to do what I think is best for him. I can't allow Brady to walk into his life out of nowhere. Not when he could just as easily walk out of it if he decides fatherhood isn't for him."

Ted nodded. "You're right, of course. I'm sure you want only the best for Max. But you underestimate Brady's motives. I only ask that you think about what it could mean for all of you before you make a final decision about this. Talk it over with Brady again."

"I'm sorry, but it's no use." She shook her head adamantly. "He's lied to me from the beginning. What guarantee do I have that he's not going to lie again?" She couldn't tell Ted about the unforgettable night she and Brady had spent together, or her pain when he'd put her aside. They weren't what her fears were about. Max's future was more important than another man passing through her life.

"None, except that you have my word Brady wouldn't deliberately do anything to hurt you or the boy."

"Brady's actions speak louder than words."

"At least let me send him back to talk to you."

"What's the use? I knew something was wrong when I asked him to tell me what was the matter. His only answer was to ask me to trust him. Trust him! Now that I know the truth of what he's been up to, I would be afraid to. For Max's sake more than mine.''

"Jenny, I..."

"No. I can't. There's no way I would be willing to take away Max's sense of security, his trust. Not even if I could offer him a father in their place. A temporary father, for all I know. How can I let a stranger walk into his life and take that security away? Or break his heart if Brady is wrong?''

"Your son loves Brady," Ted said softly, "although I'm sure you're already aware of that. If my nephew is right about being Max's father, I'm fairly certain the boy will accept him.'' He glanced over at the small rocking chair that sat in front of the television set and smiled sadly. "Indeed, from what Brady has told me about his relationship with Max, I'm sure he will.''

The fact that her son clearly loved Brady only increased her determination to protect the boy. She shook her head. "It's obvious Brady has told you I adopted Max, and about his actual parentage. My son has been told his father is in heaven with his birth mother. If we tell him Brady is his father, it will only bewilder him. If he thinks I've lied to him about something so important, how will he ever be able to believe in me again?''

"Jenny." Ted leaned across to take her hands in his. "You may be worrying needlessly. Brady sincerely believes Max is his son but, although he's tried, so far hasn't been able to prove it. Why don't you talk to him yourself, quietly and alone? You both need to find a way to locate the records of Max's parentage and settle this. I know you knew his mother, but you need to find out the truth about his biological father."

"There is no truth to find out," Jenny insisted. "As far as I'm concerned, Max's father is the one listed on his birth certificate. That's all that counts."

"I'm sure the boy's birth certificate couldn't tell you who his biological father was. But there has to be a way," he said thoughtfully. "Did Max's mother ever say which sperm bank she used?"

"No. And I wouldn't tell you if she had." Jenny looked down at the strong, capable hands that held hers. Meant to reassure her, they somehow managed to comfort her at the same time. Ted's concern over her pain was obviously genuine. She gazed into his compassionate eyes. The same appealing golden brown eyes he shared with Brady and Max. Whatever secrets he may have shared with his nephew before now, this was a man who wanted to help her, not hurt her.

"So what would *you* suggest I do now?" she asked. "How can I settle this without hurting anyone?"

"First, let me try to explain where Brady is coming from." At her reluctant nod, he patted her hand and settled back against the couch. "My nephew's family was dysfunctional, to say the least," he told her wryly. "His father may be my only brother, but I've never been able to understand how the man could place Brady in a boarding school and proceed to forget he ever had a child. Brady never lets on, but I know that must have hurt him deeply when he was a small boy. And, I'm sure, hurts him now, even though he won't admit it."

"So you're saying that after he saw Max, he wanted to be the father he never had?" She stared at Ted, unable to believe that the sight of her son had awakened Brady's latent desire for fatherhood.

"Exactly."

"He could have gotten married and had several children by now if that's what he really wanted," she retorted. "That should have been easy enough for him. Why now?"

"He's been afraid to get married, although he's never come right out and said so. That's why he's buried himself in research—statistics are easier to relate to than people. They can't abandon you or hurt you. I'm afraid my nephew has convinced himself he doesn't have what it takes to hold a wife and a child. Until now, until you, my dear."

"It's Max he wants," Jenny answered bitterly, looking down at her empty hands and remembering too much. "Not me, never me. He's only used me to get at Max."

Ted shook his head. "No, Jenny. He's too honest a man for that. He's very fond of you, I know. Maybe even more than fond, from what he tells me," he said with a whimsical smile. "And that's okay with me, too."

He rose, helped her to her feet and kissed her forehead. "I'll say good-night now. I hope you don't mind a foolish old man mixing into your life. It's only that I see and understand a bit more than you young people do.''

When she'd closed the door behind him, Jenny went back into the den and sank back onto the couch. Ted's visit had moved her, but she had concerns he couldn't possibly know about.

In the intervening years since her divorce, she gotten used to being single, focusing all her love on her son. Not until Brady had shown her how much she'd missed had she realized how lonely she actually was. Lonely for someone to share her thoughts, her dreams. A man on whom she could lavish the love stored up in her.

Brady had broken her heart; the hurt was greater than her divorce had been five years ago. She'd get over it by eventually putting this all behind her, the same way she had done once before. But mending the heart of a child? That was an entirely different matter.

Chapter Twelve

Jenny tried to, but couldn't, forget the troubled look on Brady's face when she sent him away, or the conversation she'd had with Ted Morgan last night. Yet they were nothing compared with her own anger and pain.

If, according to his uncle, Brady had ample reason to fear forming lasting relationships, he certainly had no right to try to draw her son into his life. Once he'd toyed with fatherhood, would he become dissatisfied and leave? Or was Max supposed to make up for Brady's own missing childhood?

Granted, Brady had appeared to be a perfect companion for Max. So much so, she'd begun to envision baseball games, picnics, trips to the zoo and to Disneyland. It had all seemed to fall into place so naturally; Max obviously adored Brady. And, fool that she was, she'd even begun to spin her own dreams around the man.

In spite of everything, a part of her was still in love with him.

Questions without answers swept like whirlwinds through her mind, leaving an ache that continued unabated.

It was only a matter of hours before she was to take Max to the Coopers for the weekend, before she had to face Brady and his uncle at the schoolhouse while they assembled and painted the playhouse. Now that they all shared the truth of Brady's quest, the morning was going to be sheer hell. But at least Max would be safely out of the way.

It would be a cold day in Hades before she allowed anyone to turn his happy life upside down. If anything spoiled Max's happiness, she wouldn't be able to forgive herself or anyone who caused it.

Max had done well enough without a father until now, she reasoned as she went to wake him up, although he had changed from baby to boy. She would just have to make a greater effort to expose him to "guy stuff," as Cindy was wont to say.

AT PRECISELY 8:00 a.m., after dropping off Max at the Coopers' home, she unlocked the door to the schoolhouse. The door opened and shut easily, thanks to Brady's efforts. The sign above it hung smartly horizontal, with Teddy Bear Care in painted black letters against a brown background. A smiling bear's face graced one corner, thanks to Ted. Well, she thought grimly as she entered her office, at least the two of them hadn't lied about being amateur carpenters. But Brady had lied about everything else.

This time, she was ready for him.

Inside, it was too quiet and somehow lonely without the children to keep her company. Or at least Max. She already missed his cheerful chatter, his endless questions and his sunny smile. The smile that so easily captured her heart and had led her into Brady's arms.

She was oddly grateful when she heard the sounds of Brady and Ted's arrival in front of the school. The sooner they could get started on the playhouse, the sooner they could leave. If Brady still wanted to talk, she would, but only after she put him straight about his belated attempt at fatherhood. And this time, she'd make certain he never came back again.

"Jenny? The door and gate were open so we came in."

She swung around at the sound of Brady's low, vibrant voice. How could the mere sound make her heart beat faster, her body tingle as if he'd touched her? How could the uncertain smile on his face melt the edges of her anger so quickly, even though she now knew he'd deceived her from day one?

If only he'd confided in her before he'd handed her the single, fragrant red rose. Before he'd taken her in his arms and carried her into a night filled with rapture and hope. She might have tried to understand him, even if she would never have been able to forgive him.

"Jenny, Ted told me about your conversation." Brady hesitated in the doorway as if unsure of his welcome. "I thought it would be wiser to wait until you cooled down before I came back, but Ted beat me to it.

It should have been me last night. I'd still like the chance to explain myself.''

"Explain!" she almost shouted. Anger and frustration filled her as she eyed the man she'd fallen in love with but whom she didn't dare love. "Why now, after I finally know the truth?"

"For what it's worth, I'm sorry I waited until now to tell you everything," he said as he came into the office. His eyes were cautious, his gait slow, as he took in her anger.

Good, she thought as she noted his discomfiture. He was going to be a lot sorrier when she got through with him.

"Okay for me to sit down?"

"No," she said firmly. "Say what you have to and then go put up the playhouse. As far as I'm concerned, that's the only reason you're here."

He spotted an empty chair, gestured helplessly and gazed around the office. The walls were decorated with hand-drawn crayon pictures colored by the schoolchildren. Shelves ran across the walls, containing odds and ends of animal figures and small toys near and dear to children's hearts. A large photograph of Max occupied a corner of Jenny's desk. There was a small cot in one corner of the room with a handmade patchwork quilt and a teddy bear. A hand-lettered sign above it read Comfort Corner.

The room was as warm as Jenny's gaze was cold.

"I know how upset you are," he began, holding up a hand to forestall a fresh barrage of accusations. "But

I do have my reasons.'' Her cold look was calculated to drop him in his tracks, but he started again.

"Strange as it may seem now, I backed off because I *didn't* want you to think I was using you to get at Max. I had to have the whole truth about our relationship before I told you. If Max turned out not to be my son, you would have worried for nothing. I wanted to lay my cards on the table when I had a full deck. I thought I was doing the right thing when I decided it would be more honorable to keep my distance until this was settled. I'm sorry if I hurt you.''

"'Sorry' doesn't cut it, Mr. Morgan,'' she answered curtly. "You should have thought it out more carefully. The way it's turned out, 'honor' had little to do with it. Not after you made love to me. After that night, I expected something more than distant smiles and offers to build a playhouse,'' she said. She could feel herself becoming more outraged by the moment. "And now that I've found out the truth for myself, you're finally ready to talk?''

"I'm truly sorry, Jenny,'' he apologized. "No matter what you think, I never meant to hurt you.''

"Yeah, sure,'' she snorted. "As my granny used to say, 'The road to hell is paved with good intentions.'''

Brady couldn't remember when he'd ever felt so guilty. He'd spent his life trying to do the right thing and, up until recently, had succeeded. Now, when it meant the most to him, his good intentions had blown up in his face. The look on Jenny's face told him he had almost no chance of convincing her he hadn't meant to use her, let alone that he really loved her.

"I'll leave, if you still want me to," he said when her expression turned to ice, "but before I do, I want to give you this."

He reached into his pocket and held out his open hand. In his palm lay a small rose carved out of balsa wood. "I couldn't sleep knowing how badly I've managed to bungle things. I stayed up most of the night carving this for you, Jenny. See," he said as he tried to ease the unbearable tension between them. "I painted it red so it would look like the one I gave you the other night."

The other night!

Her eyes widened as she gazed at the small, perfectly formed rose. Tiny petals had been painted a deep red, minuscule leaves a bright green. Every detail of her favorite flower was complete.

"How could you?" Her voice choked as she fought back tears. "How can you even try to keep up the charade now that I know the truth?"

"This is no charade, Jenny. I swear it." When she took a deep breath and hid her hands in her lap instead ordering him out of the office, he felt a glimmer of hope. Maybe he still had a chance with her.

"Just listen to me for a few more minutes, please."

Her glistening eyes gave her away. She looked as if she cared more than she was willing to let on. How could he convince her he understood now how much he'd hurt her by thinking only of himself? That, for a supposedly intelligent man, he realized now he'd behaved like an jerk?

"If you still want me to walk out of here once I've gotten through apologizing, I will." His knees felt like rubber when she stared at him as if he'd just crawled out of a hole in the ground. Risking her ire, he dropped into the vacant chair. He couldn't afford to mess things up again, not when there was so much at stake. The last thing he wanted was to leave without making her understand how much he loved her.

He'd intended the rose to be both a silent apology and a token of his love. He held his breath and prayed while he waited for her reaction. Had he come so close to finding the missing part of his life only to lose it now?

"Jenny?" He gently placed the little rose on the desk between them. When she glanced at the flower and back at him, her body seemed to slowly relax, her expression to change. There was a longing on her face, even though she bit her lips with seeming indecision. She wanted to believe him; he could see it in her expressive eyes.

"You do believe I love you, don't you?" he asked softly as he reached across the desk. He wanted—no, he needed—to touch her. "If not, tell me what I have to do to prove it to you."

"Maybe you just did," she answered, wiping a tear from the corner of her eye.

Their hands met across the desk, fingers reaching to touch, to hold. Their eyes were locked, hers searching, his reassuring her that he meant what he'd said.

"I do love you, Jenny," he managed through the lump in his throat. "I've never told that to anyone before. And I never will say it to anyone but you. I never meant anything so much in my life."

"I love you, too," Jenny replied in a shaky voice. "I never thought I'd say it after all that's happened in the past few days. But it's true."

He wanted to go to her, to gather her in his arms, but his rubbery knees wouldn't let him.

"Now that I'm being so honest with you," Brady said with a helpless grin, "maybe I ought to go the whole nine yards."

"True confession time?" she teased, tears still in her eyes. "What else do you have on your mind?"

He drew a deep breath, reminding himself that five minutes ago Jenny had hated the sight of him. He belatedly cursed himself for his bad timing. But, come hell or high water, the new Brady played his cards out in the open; there would be no games, not anymore. She had to know his intentions hadn't changed.

"I just have to tell you I can't walk away from the conviction that Max is my son, Jenny. I just can't."

"What do you mean?" Jenny asked, her smile fading.

"I have to prove to myself that I'm Max's biological father, but before you fly off the handle again, it has nothing to do with how I feel about you."

"What? It has everything to do with us!" Stunned, Jenny reared to her feet. If he'd taken out a gun and shot her through the heart, the results would have been the same. "Nothing has really changed, has it? If that's the way you feel, don't bother to say anything else." Her eyes narrowed and a flush came over her face. "Let me tell you, Mr. Morgan, *everything* has changed—for the worst."

"Everything, Jenny?" he asked as moved around the desk to pull her into his arms.

"Here, take this with you when you go," she said as she picked up the wooden rose and pushed it into his hands. "I don't want any part of it, and I don't want any part of you, either!"

"Jenny, please! You're wrong! The way I feel about you has nothing to do with Max."

"As far as I can tell, it has everything to do with Max," she said between set lips. "How big a fool do you think I am?" She dismissed him with a curt wave of her hand. "Don't bother to reply. The answer is obvious."

"If you really feel that way, I'm sorry," Brady said. "Maybe nothing I say or do will make a difference. But I have to explain why I think Max is my son," he said into her cold blue eyes. He stood so close to her he could feel the heat of her anger, but he wouldn't let her ignore him now.

"About five years ago, the Thurgood Institute initiated an artificial insemination program," he said slowly, carefully, as she crossed her arms over her breasts and glared at him. At least she was listening. Maybe he had a prayer of getting through his explanation with his life intact.

"At the time, its sperm bank used only donations from high IQ donors. The rationale was to raise the intellectual level of children born as the result of their program, enabling them to lead successful and productive lives. Right or wrong, I was asked to contribute."

Brady felt like a fool when Jenny raised her eyebrows. He wasn't boasting. He recalled their early arguments when Jenny insisted it was largely nurture that made well-adjusted children, not only their inherited genes. But that wasn't the point right now. There was more at stake than proving a scientific theory he wasn't that keen about, anyway.

"It's not that I claim to be a genius," he said, feeling like a fool, "but eventually I let myself be persuaded to become a donor. I swear I forgot all about my contribution until I saw you and Max being interviewed on television. His resemblance to me is so striking it hit me right between the eyes. He reminded me of a snapshot of myself taken years ago that my uncle carries in his wallet. After I checked it out, I became convinced Max was the result of that donation."

"You can't be sure about that," Jenny snapped. "You must have signed a ton of papers giving up any rights to any children born as a result of that donation. Anyway, I'm sure no reasonable man in his right mind could possibly believe a reliable bank would answer your questions or be willing to supply you with proof Max actually is your biological son!"

"*Proof?* No, not yet," he answered grimly even though he saw her growing anger. Maybe his time with

Jenny was about up, but not his determination to prove Max was his son. "Somehow I'll find it. But even without it, I know in my heart Max is my son. All you have to do is look at us. I love him already, and I can tell he feels the same way about me. He's mine, Jenny. I've never been so positive of anything in my life."

"What if you're wrong?" she questioned, coming to her feet. If looks could kill, he would have dropped dead on the spot. "What if, after you tell Max you think you're his father, you find you're not really related? Don't you realize you'd break his heart? What would happen to his trust in me, in us? He's only a vulnerable little boy. He's only four and a half years old! I can't allow you to do this to him!"

"I have no intention of hurting him, Jenny," he said quietly. "I'm convinced it would make him happy when I can tell him I'm his father. When he gets older, I'll be able to explain the whole business of artificial insemination to him. Right now he's young enough to accept me, no matter what he's been told before."

"Over my dead body!" Jenny glared at him. "And maybe not even then!"

"Won't you at least believe I honestly care for the both of you?"

"You're still out to get Max by using me, aren't you?" Jenny shook her fist under his nose until he backed away. "You're trying to soften me up so you can do it. Well, it won't work. Sorry, but I'm a lot smarter than I was three weeks ago, thanks to you. Understand?"

"You're wrong again! I'm not trying to soften you up." A sudden thought struck him—a way that would prove his good intentions and solve everything in the bargain.

"If all I wanted to do was get Max, I would have asked you to marry me before now," he said, praying she didn't have a gun in her desk, and if she did, didn't know how to shoot. "The rest would have been easy."

"You what?" Jenny became a bundle of fury at his mention of marriage. "Get out of here," she shouted. "Now!"

"Come on, Jenny. I was only trying to show you what I would have tried to do if I were the unscrupulous man you make me out to be. But I'm not. That was one of the reasons I cooled it. I didn't want you to think that was my intention."

When it looked as if her outrage hadn't softened, he went on. "I care for you more than I've cared for any woman in my life. I still want you to marry me." He ignored her sniff of disbelief and continued while he still had her attention. "And, furthermore, I don't want to 'get' Max, as you've put it. I just want to be his father, not take him away from you. You're his mother and he belongs with you. You've done a wonderful job with Max. I couldn't ask for a better mother for the boy. One thing has nothing to do with the other."

"Then go!" she commanded, pointing to the door. "Go and leave well enough alone!"

"I can't, Jenny. Be reasonable," he coaxed resisting the urge to take her in his arms and kiss her until she had stars in her eyes instead of icicles. Why couldn't she understand how important this was to him—to both of them? "I love you and I hope you'll still love me after you've had a chance to think about it."

She shook her head in denial. "No, I've had enough!"

"Even if you don't want me for yourself, Jenny, I swear to you all I want to do is share Max with you. I want to help him grow, to be a father to him. To do all the things a father does with his son. And to contribute to his support while he grows up. There's so much I want to do for him," he added, hoping against hope she'd understand how deeply he felt about being Max's father. "What more can I promise you than that?"

"He was doing fine before you," she muttered. "He doesn't need much at this age. I can handle whatever he needs by myself."

"He's growing up, Jenny. Beautifully. I thank you for that. But things will change down the line. He might need me then."

"That's a bridge I'll cross when I come to it." Jenny glanced at the red rose and pushed it away. "He doesn't need you now and neither do I."

"A boy needs his father," he insisted, biting his lips in frustration. He remembered the years without his own parents. If it hadn't been for his uncle and aunt and the summers he spent with them, he probably would have turned out to be more robot than mortal. Going through all the proper motions of being a well-adjusted human being, but empty inside. And if he allowed Jenny to call the shots, life would be empty again.

But in one way Jenny was right. He was walking proof that inheriting intelligent genes didn't cut it. Having a high IQ hadn't done a hell of a lot for him without the large doses of TLC Jenny advocated. Uncle Ted and Aunt Ellie had done what they could during summers, but there had been the long, lonely months in between visits.

He'd fooled himself for years, insisting to Ted that his absorbing scientific research was enough, and that he was content with the life he led. But that was before he'd been captured by a small boy with smiling golden eyes—and his intriguing mother.

"Look, Jenny. Maybe we can settle the whole thing reasonably." He took a deep breath and plunged right in. Things couldn't possibly be any worse than they were now. "I've been thinking of how we could resolve this dilemma. Would you allow Max's blood to be tested with mine to verify I am his father?"

Jenny's blood ran cold. "Test Max's blood with yours to see if you're his father? Are you out of your mind? Never!"

She was so upset she could hardly talk. How could he even suggest such a thing! If it turned out he *was* Max's biological father, Brady might have a greater claim on her than she did! After all, she was the one with no blood ties to Max!

She pulled herself together. She couldn't think clearly with him watching her so intently. She needed time to herself to stay one step ahead of him or she'd be in deep trouble.

"Please go now before you say anything more," she said. "Your idea may sound reasonable to you, but as far as I'm concerned it's wrong. I can't do this to Max."

"Jenny, won't you even consider it?"

"No. I don't want to hear any more about it. Your uncle is waiting for you. Put the playhouse together now that you're here. And then leave!" She gestured to the wooden rose. "Just go and take that with you."

With a long, telling look, he turned and walked out of the office, leaving the rose behind him.

Jenny glanced at the open door to make certain she was alone before she picked up the beautiful wooden flower. A tear slipped from the corner of her eye as she thought of how much she loved Brady and what might have been.

She straightened resolutely. There would be no blood tests if she could help it. Not in a million years. And if Brady thought he could force one, he had another thing coming. She'd never allow Max to be tested without a fight. No matter how long or how costly it might be.

If there was a blood match and it got as far as the courts, would a court decide to give Max to Brady? As a single mother barely making ends meet, who would the courts be sympathetic to? Would she have to give Brady visitation rights? Would Max take the Morgan name instead of hers?

She read about just such unusual legal dilemmas almost daily in the newspapers. Cases that were settled by broken hearts and lengthy court trials. Cases that were settled by law as written and without regard to the best interests of the child.

If she went along with Brady's request, would she and Max become another newspaper headline?

Chapter Thirteen

To hell with doing things the "proper" way, Brady fumed as he stormed through the empty institute and into his office just after dawn Monday morning. All his life he'd done everything the way he'd been taught, meticulously and honestly, both in his private life and in his career. But things were about to change. He looked with distaste at the immaculately-kept room that had been so carefully restored after the earthquake.

An earthquake that had transformed his life forever.

Charts covered the pristine walls, scientific journals were arranged in neat stacks in alphabetical order by name on a corner of his desk and on a bookcase behind it. A computer occupied another corner, a laser printer sat beside the desk on a cart.

Dead center on his desk was a copy of the well-publicized *The Bell Curve,* the book that claimed genetic inheritance determined a child's chances of succeeding in life. It had caused a storm since its appearance, and although definitely controversial, the theory at one time had been close to his beliefs and those of the institute. He remembered looking at it shortly before he'd left to check out Jenny and her very dissimilar ideas.

He gazed around his office with growing dislike. How in heaven's name had he found these surroundings and his statistical research so satisfying or even exciting?

Rubbing his forehead, he opened the door to his small bathroom. The private washroom marked his position in the institute's hierarchy, a position he accepted with proper modesty. He'd been proper all his life, he thought with a scowl. With not an idea or a hair on his head out of place, except for that damn shock of hair that kept falling over one eyebrow. Too proper, he thought as he combed his hair back into place with his fingers.

A glance in the mirror told him he looked like death warmed over. "And why not?" he muttered as he doused his face with cold water and briskly rubbed it dry. He'd been put through hell at least three times in the past few days. Once when he'd decided Max was his son, only to find proving it through the institute's own records impossible. Another, when Jenny had refused to have Max's blood tested and compared with his own—a test he was positive would prove he was Max's father. And the third time, when it seemed as if he'd lost Jenny herself.

He would have given anything to have another chance to do things differently.

Still cursing his luck, he used the towel to dry off the mirror and the washbasin, shook it out and hung it back neatly on the rack. After having second thoughts, he turned on the tap and splashed fresh water on the mirror and the basin. What if he *had* left drops of water on their surfaces? he thought as he rumpled the face towel and stuffed it back into the chrome rack. Such behavior would have been the kiss of death at his boarding school, but he hadn't been at boarding school for a long time. The habits pounded into him back then had become so ingrained he still acted without thinking. All that was going to change, he vowed, starting right now.

Just the way the rest of his life was changing.

He glanced down at the blue jeans, flannel plaid shirt and penny loafers he'd put on that morning without thinking twice about his choices. The shirt was open at the neck and the tie he would normally have been wearing was stuffed in a breast pocket, just in case he had to attend a meeting today.

Before he left the bathroom, he turned back, looked into the mirror and rumpled his hair.

Satisfied, he went back to his office, dropped into his comfortable executive chair and sourly regarded the journal in the center of his desk. With an oath that was unlike him, he swept it off the desk and sat back to put his mind to more constructive thinking.

He opened the briefcase he'd dropped on the floor—another uncharacteristic move, he thought proudly. If he was going to hell in a handbasket, he was determined to do it in style. Jenny would have been proud of him, too. After taking out a slightly battered Alfred, he ran his fingers over the small velour body and straightened the ear that Jenny had operated on. "Sorry, fella. I guess I forgot I put you in there last night." He propped the bear against the side of his computer. Repaired ear and all, Alfred quietly stared back at him.

Talking out loud to the bear usually helped, Brady mused. Especially when his thoughts were about Jenny. After all, Alfred knew Jenny better than he did.

"You know, Alfred, as far as I'm concerned, Max is my son. I don't need any proof. I know it just by looking at him. It just seems I'll have to find a way to prove it to the rest of the world."

Alfred's stitched black eyebrows seemed to rise a notch or two.

"I've tried to be honest in all of this," Brady explained. "Fat lot of good that's done for me," he added dryly. "Now the time has come for me to look beyond doing the right thing and get down to doing whatever will give me the answers I need. That means I have to get into Doug's program before he arrives at work. If I'm fired, so be it," he said firmly, knowing how a thief must feel just before cracking a safe.

For once, Alfred seemed to be in wholehearted agreement.

"Okay," Brady said. "As long as I have your permission . . . ." His voice trailed off as he went back to considering his computer screen.

What was the good of having a genius IQ if he couldn't figure out how to access Doug's highly secret program and dig out the data that would prove his case?

There had to be a way. It was simply a matter of putting his mind to it.

After staring at the whirling spirals of the screen saver on his computer and mulling over possibilities, Brady came wide-awake. "After all, my program and the sperm bank's are part of the institute's network, aren't they?" he asked himself softly when he noticed the weary Alfred had fallen on his side and gone to sleep.

Of course.

He grabbed a yellow lined pad and started to sketch the idea that had inched into his consciousness.

Granted, Doug locked the computer every night when he left for the day or when he wasn't around to use it. Granted, too, Doug had a password known only to him. It was simply a matter of finding it.

He tried to analyze Doug's habits. Both he and Doug had been hired in the same week and had worked together at the institute for the past ten years, although in different departments. They even met socially. He ought to know enough about the guy to be able to figure out the password Doug had chosen. The literal-minded guy couldn't have been that innovative.

When Brady had selected his own password, he'd been told not to use family names or birthdays or make any other obvious choices. After some consideration, he'd decided on *uncle,* after his Uncle Ted, the person who was closest to him.

"So, Alfred," he asked the sleeping bear, "who or what do you suppose is that important to my friend

Doug, someone or something so close to his heart he would use it for his password?''

Brady made a list of possibilities as he spoke. Names of people he knew, and even Doug's dog, Fancy.

He studied the list. They were all names Doug might have considered. But as he tried each name associated with his friend one by one, each time MESSAGE FAILED flashed across the screen.

''So, what do you think Doug really cares about, Al?'' Brady played with the keys on the keyboard. In twenty minutes, he'd exhausted all the possibilities he could think of. Damn it, he thought, why wasn't he smart enough to come up with the right password?

''The trouble with me, Alfred, is that I'm low on creativity this morning,'' he said as he leaned back and prepared to give up for the day.

Light bulbs went on in his mind, bells rang, whistles blew.

Doug was in the business of helping childless couples create life, wasn't he?

Holding his breath, Brady carefully typed the word *create* into the computer when the screen asked for his password. If this one didn't work he was dead in the water.

In seconds, the program he'd been looking for was on the screen. Even though he knew his illegal entry into the program was now a matter of record and that there would probably soon be a call from computer security, he went ahead. So what if he was hauled on the carpet, fined or thrown out of the institute? It made no difference to him now. Some things were worth more than a job with status, even if it had given him his own bathroom. A guy was entitled to prove he was a father.

ACCESS DENIED flashed across the screen. Brady was taken aback. What had he done wrong?

Of course! Like a nitwit, when asked to identify himself he'd entered his own name. This time he typed in Doug's name, praying that Doug still hadn't come in to work or turned on his computer. The computer blinked. The program came up.

Date, time, even employee serial number were requested. Luckily he knew that one. Doug's was only two digits off his. They'd joked about it often enough.

The computer digested his input for a few seconds. There on the screen in front of his eyes was the list of sperm donors, date of donation and names and addresses of recipients! Hallelujah!

A glance at his wristwatch told him it was seventwenty. He knew he had to hurry. With luck, Doug was still ten minutes behind him. If Doug followed his habit, he would arrive at the institute at precisely seven-thirty.

Hurriedly he scanned down to his own name: *Morgan, Brady*. The date he found was helpful, but not all that important as long as it was at least close to five years ago, he reasoned. It was. He let out his breath and moved the cursor across the screen and down to the next line.

In place of the name of the woman to whom his sperm would have been given was a notation: DONA-

TION NOT VIABLE. DESTROYED IN LAB. ASK DONOR TO
REPEAT.

Repeat his donation! What the hell had been wrong
with his original donation? No one had told him it had
been destroyed! Nor had anyone asked him to try again!

What the hell did "viable" mean, anyway? Was his
sperm sterile? Did it mean he couldn't be Max's father? Impossible!

Since it was something a guy was certainly entitled to
know, why hadn't he been told? Brady pressed the print
key so he could have a record for future reference.

It had to be Doug who had decided not to tell him the
bad news, he thought as he studied the printed page. He
could have tried to spare Brady the humility of knowing his sperm hadn't passed the stringent tests the institute insisted upon. Or, heaven forbid, maybe he *was*
sterile!

His panic eased when he realized that if that was the
case, he never would have been asked to repeat his donation. Not that he *had* been asked to try again, but the
rationale was comforting.

But what about Max? After spending three weeks off
and on in the kid's company, seeing for himself how
closely they resembled each other and how he felt about
the boy, how could Max *not* be his son? They looked
enough alike for Max to be a clone of his early self. He
might have been drawn by the boy's looks at first, but
he'd come to love the kid. He *was* Max's father!

A scuffling of feet behind him brought him to attention.

"Brady! What in the hell do you think you're doing?" Doug stormed into the office, a security guard at his heels.

"Trying to become a father?" Brady answered warily, turning around and eyeing the two men. He had to fight off the instinct to raise his hands in the air.

Doug, laboratory coat thrown carelessly over his shoulders, glared accusingly at the blinking cursor on Brady's computer. The guard, blue uniform sporting a discreet silver badge and a wooden club in the belt at his waist, moved in behind Brady.

Brady knew his number was up. Cautiously he backed away from the computer.

"Sorry, Doug," he apologized quickly. Hell, this was embarrassing. "But after you wouldn't answer my questions, I asked Jenny to allow Max's blood to be tested with mine. She wouldn't go along with me, either. I had to do something." He gestured at the computer. "This was my only hope. I know Max is my kid. I just wanted to be able to prove it."

Brady could feel the guard breathing down the back of his neck and realized he was inches away from being handcuffed. "How did you know it was me?"

"One of the guys in the computer security department saw the light for my computer blinking on and off. He knew someone besides me had to be trying to get into the information stored there. Yours was the only other computer in use, although my password was displayed as the user. It added up."

Doug shrugged on his lab coat and motioned to the guard to relax. "You're lucky Pete got me before coming down here. Otherwise you could have been arrested for being an industrial spy. Or were you already aware of that?"

"I knew, and frankly, I didn't care," Brady replied defiantly. "I did what I felt I had to do."

He could hear the guard stir behind him. "Tell me, do you think we could have a few moments together before Pete takes me off to jail?"

"You're not going to jail," Doug snorted, glancing at a defiant Brady, "although it's not a bad idea." He turned to the guard. "Pete, maybe you ought to go now. I'll take care of this."

"It's been recorded, you know," the guard said doubtfully. He took off his uniform cap and rubbed the back of his neck. "I'd hate to lose my job over this."

"You won't," Doug assured him. "Not when I get through explaining this mess to the boss. Brady and I will face the music when the time comes. As for you, Brady—" he glared again at his friend "—I'm not so sure."

"Well, talk fast," Doug said when the guard exited, muttering his reservation. He pulled up a chair and looked warningly at his watch. "To tell the truth, I don't know just how much time we do have. You've managed to crack a system that's highly secret and there are going to be some mighty unhappy people soon. No, on the other hand, don't tell me. I don't want to know how you did it. I'd be considered an accessory."

"Heck, it wasn't that hard," Brady said briefly. "You're not a hard man to read. And besides, you think the same way I do." His mind was in a turmoil, and now Doug was the only one who could tell him what had happened to his donation. The answer would determine what action he would take next. He handed his friend the computer printout, pointing to the entry that concerned him. "Care to explain?"

Doug studied the sheet for a moment before he tossed it back. "No wonder you're upset. I'd be worried, too, if it were me. Sorry, I don't have a clue what happened. All I know is that the sperm was viable when you donated it. The lab had to have tested it to find out if it was viable, before it was frozen for future use and its existence entered into the records. When it came time to pass it to an applicant, it must have been found unacceptable."

"Thank God for big favors! I'd hate to think I had a problem becoming a father!" Brady exclaimed, gazing at the printout. "You must be right. Something must have happened to my donation somewhere along the way because that printout says it was never issued."

"So, maybe you do have a problem, my friend, but I'm sure it has nothing to do with the viability of your donation. Unless you met Max's mother somewhere along the way five years ago, I'd say you're not a father. Not of this kid, anyway."

"I never met a woman named Marjorie, if that's your question," Brady answered. "And to my knowledge, I don't have any kids running around."

"Well, I'll leave you to your thoughts while I try to get us off the hook," Doug said as he got to his feet and started for the door. He looked back over his shoulder. "For what it's worth, friend, I wouldn't want to be in your shoes. If anyone tried to take one of my kids away from me..." He shrugged and left.

Brady righted Alfred and put him and the computer printout in his briefcase. He gazed at the computer screen with a heavy heart. He felt as though he were saying goodbye to Max, a child who'd wormed his way into his very being with that first delightful smile.

But he didn't fool himself for a minute. No matter what he'd just discovered, Jenny wouldn't want him around now anymore than she'd wanted him around before. In fact, she was less likely to have anything to do with him at all, if only because she would never be certain just what he might come up with next.

Not that he blamed her. He'd come on like a cavalry charge, befriending Max, showing Jenny how much he loved her, then, like a fool, backing off after they'd made love. What he should have done was confide in her when she'd been most likely to listen.

On the other hand, he thought wearily, the results might have been the same.

Doug's last comment to him still hung in the air. "If anyone tried to take one of my kids..." No wonder Jenny had reacted so frantically to his attempts to prove he was Max's father. She'd thought he intended to take Max away from her. Even after he'd assured her he would never do that.

Parental protective instincts obviously came with the territory. He'd been naive to expect her to welcome him with open arms after he'd asked for a blood test. He should have considered the possibility Jenny might have seen him as a threat, before he opened his mouth. Maybe he would have understood her fears if he hadn't been so anxious to have Max actually be his son.

He'd already made plans for himself and Jenny that would have taken a lifetime to fulfill. Plans that included Max and his uncle. Together, the four of them would have become a family. He and Jenny would have made a home together, perhaps even had more children to love.

No matter what he'd found in the computer records, he *had* felt like a father, and still did.

He felt a stab of regret as he prepared to leave the office and, unless he missed his guess, the institute. He was as likely to be welcome here from now on as a dead skunk on a tennis lawn. Even if Doug appealed his case.

Tears formed as he closed the office door behind him. Grown men don't cry, he told himself as he walked out of the institute, but he couldn't help it. His dreams had collapsed like a house of cards.

He'd grabbed for the gold ring and missed.

He'd find a new life for himself somehow. But how could he say goodbye to Jenny and her son without losing a part of himself in the bargain?

Chapter Fourteen

Once Brady was outside in the cold morning air, his head seemed to clear. The next step in resolving his problem became obvious. He had to confront Jenny, make her believe he loved her, that she was the most important person in his life. And to agree, no matter how badly he'd bungled their relationship, that they belonged together. He intended to take care of it before another day passed.

As for Max actually being his son, what made a father anyway?

It was certainly more than biological ties. He could testify to that. His own father had contributed his genes and not much else. Even during his infrequent visits home, he hadn't shown more than a passing interest in him when he was growing up, and not much more than that now, either.

One of the things he wanted for Max was a home with a loving mother and father in it three hundred sixty-five days a year. No, he corrected himself as he strode to his car, three hundred sixty-six if he counted leap year.

Sure, that was his dream, yet dreams took more than wishes. Jenny had taught him that raising a kid was demanding work and the perfect family was impossible. He was a long way from being perfect, but Jenny was close.

In a way he felt a profound sense of relief that the ties that bound him to Max weren't biological and that he had no claim on the boy. Only the love he bore him. Once Jenny understood that his ties to Max were a matter of heart to heart, maybe she'd forgive him. Maybe then she'd realize that he loved her for herself and not just for Max's sake.

HE ARRIVED at the school at lunchtime after ignoring every speed-limit sign along the way. That was out of character for him, too, but then everything he seemed to do lately was out of character.

Overhead, dark clouds were rolling in across the valley, and a mist had begun to fall. The playground was empty; the newly painted red playhouse glistened. In typical February fashion, what had started out to be a pleasant morning threatened to become a cool afternoon.

That meant the children would be inside—sort of an insurance policy that his visit would be received without undue comment from Jenny.

Maybe at first she wouldn't be happy to see him, but he was here to stay no matter what. And with eighteen pairs of eyes and ears watching and listening, she would have no choice but to be polite.

THE DOORBELL RANG. With a glance at Jenny, Cindy went to the door and opened it.

"Hi, Cindy!" Brady traded smiles with the star-struck young girl. When she held the door open for him to come inside, he felt strangely as if he were coming home.

Jenny glanced up from where she was helping Tommy unwrap his peanut butter-and-jelly sandwich. She frowned when she saw Brady. Drat! She'd forgotten to tell Cindy that Brady was no longer welcome. But from the foolish smile on Cindy's face as she followed in Brady's wake, Jenny guessed it would have been a lost cause anyway. It wasn't Cindy's fault. Brady's smile was irresistible; she'd been its target often enough to know.

She watched him weave his way through excited children, stopping now and then to shake an eager hand or accept a gift of a cookie. The man was a regular Pied Piper the way children took to him.

As for Max, she wondered whether maybe, just maybe, Brady might have a point about biological inheritance. If he was Max's father, did she have the moral right to keep them apart?

Of course she did! Brady had given up his rights to any child of his when he'd signed a piece of paper. She'd been the one to care for, love and nurture Max from the first moment she'd laid eyes on him. The bond between her and her son was what counted, she assured herself.

By the time he reached Jenny, Brady could tell her blood was boiling. That was all right with him. His blood was boiling, too, but for a different reason.

"What are you doing here?" she asked beneath her breath when he finally joined her. "I thought you understood I told you never to come back!"

"I never say 'never,'" he answered casually over Max's head when Max jumped up to grasp him around the knees. "It's not in my vocabulary. Neither is the word *quitter*."

"Hi, Mr. Morgan!" Max said happily, raising his face for a welcome kiss. "Are we going to fix something else today?"

"You might say so," Brady answered, hugging the boy and avoiding Jenny's icy glare. He wiped a smudge of peanut butter off the tip of Max's nose with a paper napkin from a stack in the middle of the table. "But this time, it's a one-man job. And I figure I'm just the man to take care of it." He glanced expectantly at Jenny. Her cold expression hadn't changed.

"Aw, Mr. Morgan," Max pleaded. "Can't I help? Please? I have my toolbox here!"

"Next time, sport. This time, it's a job for a grown man," Brady said firmly. "But you figure in my future plans in a big way."

"Promise?"

"Promise," Brady agreed with a final hug before he looked up at Jenny. She was watching him with a jaundiced eye, but at least she kept her tongue. Though if looks could kill . . .

"Something wrong?" Brady asked innocently. He knew full well his question would open the door to a torrent of accusations, but accusations were something he was prepared to handle. Thank goodness the kids were close by; he hated to think what her reaction might have been if he'd arrived when the children were outside or sleeping.

"You bet. Something is *definitely* wrong," she replied in a tight voice after she managed to turn the kids' attention back to their lunches. "What are you doing here?"

"I wanted to talk to you," he said simply. "And I couldn't wait."

"And I told you I wanted you out of my life," she retorted. "If I never saw you again it would be too soon!"

"I thought you wouldn't mind if I'd dropped in for lunch," he stated, showing her a paper bag with the McDonald's logo on it.

"You didn't!" she said.

"I admit I used to shy away from fast foods," he said, a sheepish look on his face. "Except that you might say recently I've become hooked on McDonald's."

A cold silence was his answer. At his quirked eyebrow, she clenched her fists and started for her office. "Come with me," she said over her shoulder. "It looks as if we need to clarify this situation once and for all."

"You're absolutely right," Brady agreed as he dropped the paper bag in front of Max and put a finger to his lips. "Cookies," he explained in a whisper before he waved goodbye and followed Jenny.

Now he would have her all to himself, he thought as he followed Jenny. And where he could make her understand how much she meant to him without the world of small children listening. After that, and only after that, he'd make her see that he considered Max his son, biology be damned.

"I guess you didn't understand me the other day," Jenny remarked testily. She waited until he came into the office, then gestured for him to close the door behind him. "Unless you have another subject to talk about besides me and Max, which I doubt, I want you out of my life!"

Not as badly as he wanted to be in it, he thought as Jenny put the desk between them.

"I came to tell you what I managed to dig out of the institute's computer records," he offered as he seated himself in the chair in front of her desk. He was there for the duration, and this time he wasn't going to ask for permission. He was going to clear the air.

"I thought that was a closed book," she said suspiciously. "How did you... My goodness, you didn't hack into their program, did you?" she asked as she regarded him with disbelief.

"Sorry to disappoint you, but yes, I did." He leaned back in the chair, folded his arms across his chest and waited for a lecture on white-collar crime. "It was simply a question of going ahead with what I felt I had to do."

"That's illegal," she announced, glancing around as if she was afraid the walls had ears. "But I'm not surprised. You certainly aren't the man I thought you were the first time I laid eyes on you. You looked like you were an honest man. Now you're telling me you've done something criminal! Don't you know you can go to jail for doing something like that!"

"And would you care if I did?"

"Not at all. At least I'd get you out of my life," she answered, fixing him with a cold look. "Still, I wouldn't want anyone to go to jail for anything I might have indirectly caused."

No matter what she'd said in anger before now, he was relieved to think Jenny still cared about him.

"Well, now that you know I tapped into the institute's records, you might as well know the whole story." He had her undisguised interest now.

"I'm not sure I want to know," she said warily, eyeing him with a frown. "Somehow I think I'm not going to like what you have to say anymore than I liked your suggestion about a blood test."

"On the contrary," he said, feeling a rush of elation now that he was getting closer to having her listen to him without her launching into another tirade. Not that he didn't have it coming, but he was trying to tell her he was sorry. "You're going to love this story."

"Are you sure you want to tell me? I might use your confession against you, you know," she threatened.

"I'll take the chance. Besides, I'm looking forward to having you help me with the ending."

"You have just about ten more minutes before I help the kids clean up and get them settled down for their naps," she warned. "So, Mr. Morgan, what's the story?"

"It won't take long." He drew a deep breath. "When I went down to the institute bright and early this morning, I realized my own computer and the computer with the sperm-bank records in it were on the same network. It took a little time for me to come up with the proper password, but I managed to do it. I found everything I wanted to know. And a few things I didn't want to know," he amended. "That was before I got caught."

"Were you arrested?"

"Not quite," Brady admitted. "Actually, I left while the leaving was good."

Jenny's eyes widened as she listened to his story. "You sure were taking a chance. I thought hacking your way into someone else's private files was a federal offense!"

"No," he assured her solemnly. "I confined myself to the institute's donor files. After all, I worked for the same institution. It wasn't as if I entered some other organization's records."

"'Worked'?" she asked. How unlike the old Brady to get himself fired. As for the new Brady...well, doing something like that wasn't beyond the realm of possibility. "What do you mean 'worked'? Don't you still work there?"

"Well," he began, "I'm not sure. It will depend on whether the guy who's in charge of the program is willing to understand my motives and is prepared to let it go."

"I'm not sure I understand your motives, either."

"Probably not," he said agreeably, "but I hope you will before I'm through. Anyway, I found the answer to my question. I know what happened to my...er..." He hesitated before he found the word that wouldn't start an argument. "Donation."

"And?"

Her face had already become tinged with a charming pale-pink blush as she followed his story. Now it was positively pink.

"It turned out it wasn't viable and was ultimately destroyed," he said calmly.

She sucked in her breath. "Are you telling me that you are *not* Max's father?"

"Right." He nodded gravely. "I am definitely not Max's biological father."

He crossed his fingers under the desk. He was telling her the truth, but not the whole truth. Max *was* his son, as far as he was concerned.

There was no substitute for the reasoning of the human heart.

Jenny all but collapsed in relief. "Thank goodness for that," she muttered.

She studied Brady for a moment. He met her gaze openly, wishing that she could see all the way into the depths of his soul. Then she was cocking her head and giving him that teacher look.

"How come you sound so happy about being proved wrong? I would have thought you'd be miserable now that you know Max isn't your biological son."

"No." He glanced over at Max's framed picture with a faint smile. "I'd already decided it doesn't really matter."

Her gaze followed his to the photo. She studied it for a moment, then turned back to him. "How do you account for Max looking just like you?"

"I guess it was just luck."

"Good. Now maybe you can forget the whole idea and get on with your life." She started to rise, but the expression on Brady's face stopped her.

"That's precisely what I intend to do," Brady assured her. "And that's what I wanted to talk to you about."

"What do I have to do with the rest of your life?" she asked warily. Although she kept her face blank, her heart felt as if it had sunk to her knees, leaving an empty space behind. Just the thought of never seeing Brady again left a hollow feeling in her chest and, as their eyes locked, an ache that grew as big as a mountain. How was she going to get by without him? Never to see his shy, lopsided smile, the poignant way he'd fallen in with her teddy bear fantasies; never to have him bring her another rose...

Never again to feel his arms around her, his lips on hers, his warm skin sliding against hers as he made love with her?

These were all images that exploded in her mind. No matter what she'd told Brady, she didn't know how she could continue to live without them.

"I want you to consider marrying me," he said simply. "No," he amended as he reached across the desk to take her hand. "Don't stop to consider it. Just say yes."

"So you can have Max?" she said in a whisper, more to herself than him. Why else would he tell her he wasn't her son's father if he didn't still intend to be a father to Max, one way or another?

"No, Jenny," he replied, "so I can have you."

"What about Max?" She wasn't all that convinced this wasn't a ruse to suck her into forgiving him in order for him to get Max.

"He can come along, too," he assured her with a faint smile. "As a matter of fact, I feel as though he's already mine in all the ways that count."

She'd never seen Brady so solemn, so earnest.

"See," he went on as he laid his open palms on the desk. "I came to here today with clean hands. No charades, no subterfuge. I came here with only the simple truth, no hidden agendas. I came to ask you to trust in me, and, if you do, to marry me for my sake. I need you. I don't want to imagine what my life would become without you."

Tears of happiness mingled with uncertainty filled Jenny's eyes. She couldn't imagine what life would be without him, either. "Me?"

"You have to let me be your man, Jenny, because already I feel that I am. If you don't believe I'll be a good husband, I'll take lessons, I promise."

"You promise a lot of things, don't you?" she asked with a watery smile.

"And I always keep my promises," he answered, getting to his feet. He came around the desk and lifted her into his arms. "Ask Max if you don't believe me."

He moved to the rocking chair she had placed next to the little cot in the Comfort Corner that morning and dropped into it with her in his arms. She was trying to consider his question. He deserved a thoughtful response, but it was hard to think clearly with his arms around her. The sweet, devilish curve of his mouth was too distracting.

"Jenny?" he asked when the silence went on too long to suit him.

"I'm trying to answer you," she replied, digging in a little closer to him. Tears started at the corners of her eyes when he tightened his hold. He was solid and tantalizing and all hers, if she wanted him.

"It seems to me you could use a little tender, loving care yourself, sweetheart," he murmured into her ear before he wiped away her tears with a gentle finger. Then he kissed her gently on her forehead, her cheeks and, finally, on her lips.

The kiss became stronger as he sought the taste of her. With a deep sigh of relief, she gave in to what she longed to do. She put her arms around his neck and kissed him with all the love she had within her.

He was her dream come true, a man so special she'd given up trying to find him. The past vanished in a whirlpool of passion as he held her to him and kissed her deeply. She could feel the beat of his heart, the heat of his desire, through his shirt. Her heart seemed to join his as she returned his kiss.

An eternity later, he loosened his hold on her but held her against his chest and rested his chin on her hair while his heart returned to its normal beat.

"Does that mean a yes?" he finally inquired.

"It does," she answered, turning her face up to his. "But first we'll have to ask Max if it's okay with him."

As if right on cue, the door opened cautiously and Max peeked around it.

"Mommy?"

"It's okay. Come in," Brady said when Max's golden brown eyes opened wide in wonder at seeing him in the rocking chair with Jenny in his arms.

"Don't you feel good, Mommy?" Max asked, small worry lines creasing his forehead.

"Your mother just needed a little hug to make her feel better and I knew just how to do it," Brady replied with a broad smile. "In fact, if you have a minute to spare, you might just come over here. There's room enough for you, too."

"Gosh, Mr. Morgan," Max said as he inched into the room to stand in front of Brady. "You sure know how to fix a lot of things, don't you?"

Jenny laughed and held out her arms. "Come here, sweetheart. We have something to tell you," she said. "Mr. Morgan and I have decided to get married. What do you have to say about that?"

Max quivered with excitement as he thought about the question. His eyes lit up and he started to dance. "Does that mean he's going to be my dad?"

"You bet, if you'll have me," Brady answered for Jenny.

He'd loved Max from the first time the kid had looked up at him with those innocent brown eyes. A desire for fatherhood had been planted in Brady's heart at that moment and grown until he realized how desperately he wanted to be a father. And that desire had been nourished by that quirky little smile ever since. A smile that, for whatever the reason, they both shared.

As far as he was concerned, the bond between them had been cemented the first time he'd held that small, trusting hand in his.

"Is that what you meant when you said you were going to let me be in your future plans?" Max asked as Jenny put her arms around him.

The kid was as smart as a whip, Brady thought as he nodded. Whoever had been his father must have been quite a guy. Brady sensed he was going to have a lot to live up to.

"Sure. I just didn't know they were going to include you and your mother so soon. But I was hoping," he said as he nuzzled Jenny's sweet-smelling hair.

"Does that mean I can have some sisters and brothers, too, Mr. Morgan?"

"First things first, sport. Your mother and I have to get married. We'll take care of that as soon as we can, and as soon as we get my Uncle Ted wired in. And maybe," Brady said, looking to Jenny for approval, "you can call me 'Dad' instead of 'Mr. Morgan.' That is, if you really want to."

"Wow!" Max replied, jumping up and down and waving his arms. "Do I! This is better than Christmas! I'm going to tell Tommy!"

Before they could stop him, he was out the door. They could hear him shout "Hey, Tommy! Guess what? I'm going to have a Dad of my very own!"

"Do you suppose we could have a few more just like Max?" Brady asked, smiling into Jenny's sparkling eyes.

"I'd need to have a daughter or two to even the score," Jenny answered. "I have a feeling you and Max will be a tough act to beat."

"You'd better believe it," Brady answered as he returned to the task of comforting Jenny. "Though maybe next time, with a little luck, the child will look just like you."

BRIDE'S BAY RESORT

UNLOCK THE DOOR TO GREAT ROMANCE AT BRIDE'S BAY RESORT

Join Harlequin's new across-the-lines series, set in an exclusive hotel on an island off the coast of South Carolina.

Seven of your favorite authors will bring you exciting stories about fascinating heroes and heroines discovering love at Bride's Bay Resort.

Look for these fabulous stories coming to a store near you beginning in January 1996.

Harlequin American Romance #613 in January
Matchmaking Baby by Cathy Gillen Thacker

Harlequin Presents #1794 in February
Indiscretions by Robyn Donald

Harlequin Intrigue #362 in March
Love and Lies by Dawn Stewardson

Harlequin Romance #3404 in April
Make Believe Engagement by Day Leclaire

Harlequin Temptation #588 in May
Stranger in the Night by Roseanne Williams

Harlequin Superromance #695 in June
Married to a Stranger by Connie Bennett

Harlequin Historicals #324 in July
Dulcie's Gift by Ruth Langan

Visit Bride's Bay Resort each month wherever Harlequin books are sold.

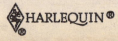

HARLEQUIN ®

BBAYG

Take 4 bestselling love stories FREE

Plus get a FREE surprise gift!

Special Limited-time Offer

Mail to Harlequin Reader Service®

3010 Walden Avenue
P.O. Box 1867
Buffalo, N.Y. 14240-1867

YES! Please send me 4 free Harlequin American Romance® novels and my free surprise gift. Then send me 4 brand-new novels every month, which I will receive months before they appear in bookstores. Bill me at the low price of $3.12 each plus 25¢ delivery and applicable sales tax, if any.* That's the complete price and a savings of over 10% off the cover prices—quite a bargain! I understand that accepting the books and gift places me under no obligation ever to buy any books. I can always return a shipment and cancel at any time. Even if I never buy another book from Harlequin, the 4 free books and the surprise gift are mine to keep forever.

154 BPA A3UM

Name	(PLEASE PRINT)	
Address		Apt. No.
City	State	Zip

This offer is limited to one order per household and not valid to present Harlequin American Romance® subscribers. *Terms and prices are subject to change without notice. Sales tax applicable in N.Y.

UAM-696   ©1990 Harlequin Enterprises Limited

HARLEQUIN®

A M E R I C A N ◆ R O M A N C E®

American Romance is about to ask that most important question:

Where were you when the lights went out?

When a torrid heat wave sparks a five-state blackout on the Fourth of July, three women get caught in unusual places with three men whose sexiness alone could light up a room! What these women do in the dark, they sure wouldn't do with the lights on!

Don't miss any of the excitement in:

#637 NINE MONTHS LATER...
By Mary Anne Wilson
July 1996

#641 DO YOU TAKE THIS MAN...
By Linda Randall Wisdom
August 1996

#645 DEAR LONELY IN L.A....
By Jacqueline Diamond
September 1996

Don't be in the dark—read
WHERE WERE YOU WHEN THE LIGHTS WENT OUT?—
only from American Romance!

BLACKOUT

HARLEQUIN® AMERICAN ROMANCE®

Maybe This Time...

Maybe this time...they'll get what they really wanted all those years ago. Whether it's the man who got away, a baby, or a new lease on life, these four women will get a second chance at a once-in-a-lifetime opportunity!

Four top-selling authors have come together to make you believe that in the world of American Romance anything is possible:

#642 ONE HUSBAND TOO MANY
Jacqueline Diamond
August

#646 WHEN A MAN LOVES A WOMAN
Bonnie K. Winn
September

#650 HEAVEN CAN WAIT
Emily Dalton
October

#654 THE COMEBACK MOM
Muriel Jensen
November

Look us up on-line at: http://www.romance.net

MTTG

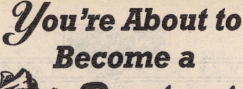

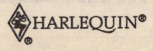